Dedalus Euro S
General Edito

My Little Husband

Pascal Bruckner

My
Little
Husband

Translated by Mike Mitchell

Dedalus

Dedalus would like to thank the French Ministry of Culture in Paris for its assistance in producing this book and Arts Council, England for its support of the Dedalus publishing programme.

Supported using public funding by
**ARTS COUNCIL
ENGLAND**

Published in the UK by Dedalus Limited,
24-26, St Judith's Lane, Sawtry, Cambs, PE28 5XE
email: info@dedalusbooks.com
www.dedalusbooks.com

ISBN printed book 978 1 909232 31 0
ISBN ebook 978 1 909232 59 4

Dedalus is distributed in the USA & Canada by SCB Distributors,
15608 South New Century Drive, Gardena, CA 90248
email: info@scbdistributors.com   web: www.scbdistributors.com

Dedalus is distributed in Australia by Peribo Pty Ltd.
58, Beaumont Road, Mount Kuring-gai, N.S.W. 2080
email: info@peribo.com.au

Publishing History
First published in France in 2007
First Dedalus edition in 2013
First ebook edition in 2013

Mon Petit Mari © Editions Grasset & Fasquelle 2007
Translation copyright © Mike Mitchell 2013

The right of Pascal Bruckner to be identified as the author & Mike Mitchell to be identified as the translator of this work has been asserted by them in accordance with the Copyright, Designs and Patents Act, 1988.

Printed in Finland by Bookwell
Typeset by Marie Lane

The Author

Pascal Bruckner is best known as a controversial philosopher. Two of his essays – *The Tyranny of Guilt* and *Perpetual Euphoria: On the duty to be Happy* were published to great acclaim in English translation in 2011 and 2012.

He has won two major French prizes for his fiction: *The Prix Medicis* and *The Prix Renaudot*.

His novel *Lunes de fiel* was made into the film *Bitter Moon* by Roman Polanski.

The Translator

For many years an academic with a special interest in Austrian literature and culture, Mike Mitchell has been a freelance literary translator since 1995. He is one of Dedalus's editorial directors and is responsible for the Dedalus translation programme. He has published over seventy translations from German and French.

His translation of Rosendorfer's *Letters Back to Ancient China* won the 1998 Schlegel-Tieck Translation Prize after he had been shortlisted in previous years. His translations have been shortlisted three times for The Oxford Weidenfeld Translation Prize: *Simplicissimus* by Johann Grimmelshausen in 1999, *The Other Side* by Alfred Kubin in 2000 and *The Bells of Bruges* by Georges Rodenbach in 2008.

His recent translations include *Where Tigers Are At Home* by Jean-Marie Blas de Roblès and *The Lairds of Cromarty* by Jean-Pierre Ohl.

For Anna
in memory of the day
when we encountered the little husband.

My father said I must be wed,
My God, what a man, what a little man,
My God, what a man, he might as well be dead,
I've lost him in my great big bed!
My God, what a man, what a little man,
I've lost him in my great big bed,
My God, what a man, he might as well be dead…

(17th-century French song)

I want to have a spouse,
A man that's nice and small,
Ever at my beck and call,
A proper little spouse,
A mannikin for the house,
As docile as a mouse
Who'll never disagree –
Like Daddy used to be.
At home I'll have the say,
Do things in my own way.
I'll do just as I please,
It's me who makes the rules,
If he objects – hard cheese!

(19th-century French song)

When Léon and Solange entered the church everyone was struck by the difference in height between them. Even though he was wearing heel inserts and held himself ramrod-straight, he still only came to just above her shoulder. But no one was bothered by it, neither the pious old maids muttering behind their missals nor Solange's family. The contrast had been a shock at first, but now it was blurred by the good qualities of their future son-in-law. It showed broadness of mind for a woman to fall in love with a man shorter than she was when the converse had been the rule so far. It was seen as a happy omen: male superiority finally brought down a peg. A small man could marry an amazon, a lady of mature years could lust after a younger man. The prejudices of former times were disappearing.

It helped that Léon, with his black hair thrown back in the Romantic style, cut a handsome figure. With his big, blue-grey eyes, long face and full lips he did Solange proud. She was a magnificent creature, tall and full-bosomed with a redhead's glowing complexion. Solange's imposing décolletage filled with lilies and her broad, suntanned and half-naked back meant that her progress down the aisle on her father's arm was accompanied by murmurs of astonishment. Even the priest felt his blood stir and had to keep his eyes down in order to perform his office. To be honest, Léon wasn't that short, five foot six inches is still respectable, it was Solange who went over the top with her full six feet. It was quite a difference. But the couple had transformed the disparity into an asset, almost a mark of distinction.

Léon was crazy about his wife. He showered her with presents, and surrounded her with attention and little marks of affection. Being very pious, she had stood firm in refusing to allow them to yield sooner to their mutual desire, insisting on a proper engagement before the wedding. For a whole year she had kept his passion on a low flame. Full of the joy of being courted, she only granted him minor favours, too slight to be immoral but with sufficient promise to stoke his fire. On the wedding day, after the priest had asked the ritual questions, reminded the couple of their duty to be faithful, to keep each other in sickness and in health, and dealt with the rings, Léon stood up on the tips of his toes to plant a kiss on Solange's lips. She, unable to lean down for fear of spoiling her long white dress and losing the circlet of flowers over her forehead, had to grasp him round the waist to lift him up to her mouth. In her hands he seemed light as a feather, literally walking on air a couple of inches off the ground. The assembled guests, moved by this tender gesture, applauded.

Part 1

Love with Dire Consequences

1

Communicating Vessels

They set up home in one of the central districts of Paris, not far from the Bastille, facing some public gardens, and they took an apartment with a balcony on the sixth floor in order to have an open view. Solange's parents, prudent shopkeepers who had put away a tidy sum, lent them the deposit for the mortgage. The young couple, just into their thirties, put themselves in debt to the banks for the next twenty years at an attractive rate of interest. Solange, an only child, had sailed through her studies, qualifying at the age of twenty-nine as a dental surgeon specialising in traumas of the jaw. While waiting to set up her own surgery, she was working for a colleague and was highly regarded by her patients for her skill at treating them painlessly. Léon, an orphan from the age of four, had lived on social security and scholarships. He had got to know Solange at university where he had specialised in otolaryngology, with equally outstanding results. The connections between their specialisms brought them even closer together.

How did they deal with their respective sizes, how did they go about it? That was their business and theirs alone. It didn't stop them from being the most radiant of couples. Being seen with this dazzling valkyrie in tow brought Léon the female sympathy vote on numerous occasions, but he paid no attention to it; the splendour of Solange put all potential rivals in the shade. He didn't even see them, his sole ambition was to love his lawful wedded wife and to inseminate her as often as she wished. The males of their acquaintance were outraged at the idea of this little runt sharing the bed of such a beauty, but the couple were completely impervious to their banter.

Statistics tell us that tall, self-assured men are what women prefer. Solange was not one of them: her little doctor was all she could wish for. She set a cracking pace for him, he had to take three steps to every two of hers which, at the end of the day, amounted to several hundred extra steps. She never slowed down, and so he got into the habit of scurrying along beside her, slightly out of breath. When travelling, he would trot behind her carrying the suitcases while she strode along, head held high, not looking round. On certain evenings, when she'd had the odd drink, she would take Léon on her knee, calling him my Lion, my Magnificent Stallion, all the while teasing and tickling him. He gave himself up to it like a little boy, squirming, legs squeezed tight together in mock embarrassment. Perhaps because he'd lost his parents very young, Léon dreamt of a large family. He loved children above all, they were his passion, his *raison d'être*. The wailing of a newborn child and a warm glance from a little urchin made up for all the indignities of life.

He performed his marital duties so assiduously that nine months to the day after their nuptials Solange was delivered of a boy, Baptiste, a strapping brat of almost ten pounds with bright red cheeks, bawling like a barracks bugle. Well, well, he certainly took after his mother as far as physique and sound level were concerned! Generally during pregnancy husbands are relegated to second place, confronted with a mystery which is beyond them. That was not at all the case here. Together with his wife, Léon had experienced every little aspect of gestation, feeling with her the foetus kicking, suffering the contractions.

His stomach, thanks to a special talent for distension, had managed to swell up to the size of his wife's. It looked like a wineskin or an amphora.

For a whole week Léon never took his eyes off the little marvel, who they installed in a little room with pink and blue wallpaper and a cradle with a canopy. A wooden stork, hanging from a gold thread over the cot, gently flapped its wings at the least breath of air. Heavy cretonne curtains shielded the infant's sleep, creating a soft half-light during his siestas.

Léon was so proud he had to restrain himself from stopping people in the street and declaring, 'Just imagine, I'm a father!' He rang up his friends, even those who lived far away, to tell them the news, and had pinned up photos of the baby all over the walls of his office.

To celebrate the birth, the new parents acquired a little black-grey-and-white cat, which they christened Furbelow, hoping it would soon be a playmate for their son. As a modern father, Léon insisted on doing his share of the chores, getting up during the night to wipe the baby's bottom, clean him up and change his nappy, while Solange, generously endowed, suckled him every three hours, graciously allowing her husband to gather the last drops that the little darling, having drunk his fill, rejected. For Léon there was nothing sweeter than to make a fuss of his little pink cherub. He wasn't disgusted by anything, not by slobber, nor by wee-wee or poo. Everything about Baptiste was magical, his googoos had the beauty of an epic poem. He couldn't wait for Solange to recover from her confinement so that he could serve her again. Once the conventional period of abstinence had been observed, he threw himself into her arms and sowed his seed abundantly. Wherever they were, whatever the time, they didn't go to sleep without a vigorous cuddle.

Six weeks after the birth of Baptiste, Léon, putting on his corduroy jacket, the one he wore when they were going out into the country, noticed that the sleeves had stretched and came half way down his fingers while the shoulders drooped more than usual.

'Shit! And I had it made to measure. I'll have to take it back to the tailor.'

He took another jacket out of the wardrobe – with the same result. It too seemed to have grown during the night, and the ends of the sleeves dangled down as if his arms were mere stumps. He started to laugh. What was going on? Was someone playing a joke on him? Ok then, he'd tuck up the sleeves and put on a sweater underneath to bulk out his chest and shoulders. But then when he tried his black slip-ons his feet were lost inside them and his toes didn't reach to the end any more. Furious, he stuffed some newspaper into his shoes and went out with the strange feeling of having put on his big brother's clothes.

Even though he'd decided to ignore the problem, he couldn't help feeling slightly disturbed. He ran through various hypotheses, each crazier than the last: as a practical joke Solange had replaced his clothes with other, similar ones which were just a little bit bigger. But why should she play a trick like that on him? She'd never made anything of her superior height. She had chosen him from among all the others according to the principle that small is beautiful. A mistress of euphemism, she had banished words such as 'dwarf', 'midget' and 'half-pint' from her vocabulary and asked her guests to abide by that rule. She even regarded exclamations such as 'You could have knocked me down with a feather!' as bad form.

Léon decided not to mention it to her. There would always

be time for that. But two days later, when they were going out to see friends, there was another incident. They were standing in the lift, which had a large tinted mirror at the back, when Solange suddenly exclaimed, 'Léon, you scatterbrain, you've forgotten to put your shoes on! Got your head in the clouds again, I suppose.'

Léon quivered. Not only had he not forgotten to put his shoes on, he'd supplemented his heel inserts with two extra inches of leather sole.

'Look at yourself in the mirror, you great ninny.'

'I assure you I am wearing them, Solange.'

He bowed his head in embarrassment and showed her his feet, duly enveloped in black, polished chukka boots with platform soles. Since he'd met Solange, Léon kept his shoes on at all times, even on the beach, where he wore reinforced flip-flops, thick as twelve-ounce steaks. His slippers had a cork insert to make them higher. Solange for her part had decreed an inviolable law: no platform soles while they were making love. He was allowed to put them back on afterwards.

'But what's going on, then?' Solange said. 'Have I perhaps mistakenly put on some stiletto heels?'

No. Solange, ever tactful, never wore them when she was with Léon. She kept them for private hen parties, when she teetered along on high-heeled shoes that made her husband feel dizzy. It was the evening of 17 July, and she was wearing the flattest of flat sandals with paper-thin soles, ideal for summer walks.

'But what's happened to you, darling? I don't understand.'

That was how the tragedy arrived, without warning, like all tragedies, ushered in by an innocuous incident. It was a dismal evening for Léon, even if no one said anything to upset him apart from their hosts' little girl who buzzed round him exasperatingly, repeating, 'Hey, you've changed, you've changed.'

People had become used to his lack of height. He was subjected to some mild teasing, but most of the couple's friends were over six foot and focused their attention and admiration on his amazing auburn-haired wife. He merely served as a foil, like a zebra placed beside a giraffe. They commiserated with her, they chaffed her – after all, she'd asked for it.

The next day he went out straight away and bought some special orthopaedic shoes. They were very inconvenient for walking, but they gave him an extra seven inches of height. He normally took six and a half, but the assistant assured him his size was at most six, in fact more like five and a half.

'Are you sure? Check again.'

She confirmed the size was indeed five and a half. It hit him like a piece of terrible news and he put his head in his hands.

'Did I say something silly?' the salesgirl asked. 'Have I offended you? I'm terribly sorry, I'll give you a pair of sixes if you like, but they'll be less comfortable, your feet'll be flopping around inside them. You'll risk getting blisters or twisting your ankle.'

All his clothes hung loose on him and, with a heavy heart, Léon had to have them taken in and the sleeves and legs shortened, the collars adjusted, five extra holes made in his belts and the elastic of his underpants – they were falling down round his thighs, indeed, down to his calves – tightened. As for the rest of his clothes, and despite the nuisance, he got used to living with socks that were too long and came up to his crotch, trousers that flapped round his legs, shirts that were too big and looked like doctors' coats and T-shirts as voluminous as a bathing-wrap. At work, where they noticed the broadening rather than the shortening effect, they thought he was trying to disguise the beginnings of a spare tyre; his penchant for roomy clothes was, they felt, not without a certain style. They were careful not to make any comments and their discretion reassured him.

2

What's in a Few Inches?

At first he thought Fate was playing a joke on him. After all, there was nothing wrong with seeing the world from a bit lower down. Every evening he went to sleep convinced he would wake up in the morning to find everything was back to normal again. But the respite was brief, the little joke was threatening to turn into a shaggy-dog story. One Wednesday morning, after a terrible storm during the night had freshened the air, Solange didn't recognise Léon when he got up.

'Stop playing the fool and walking on your knees,' she said sharply. 'Stand up.'

Poor Léon. All he could do was to show her his legs, for he was already dressed, right down to his shoes, and was standing up stiff as a poker so as not to lose the least fraction of an inch. The subterfuge with the orthopaedic shoes wasn't working any more. He looked pitiful in trousers concertinaing down onto shoes that could have accommodated two feet like his. This time something had definitely happened.

'Léon! You're getting smaller! What have you been eating?' Solange cried out in concern.

That same day they made an appointment with the family doctor, who referred them to a specialist in growth problems and endocrinology. This was Professor Daniel Dubbelviz, a chubby fifty-year-old giant who always wore a bow tie, was easy-going and devastatingly good-humoured. He examined

Léon carefully, measured his height, weighed him, took a urine sample and a blood sample. His diagnosis was a premature collapse of the spinal column.

'At thirty-one you're going through what many men go through after they've reached seventy or seventy-five. It's a staggering example of precocious senility. But don't worry, I'll get you back on track. I guarantee you'll recover at least two to three inches in height within a year.'

'How?'

'I'm going to shore you up like a sapling, fix a support to your back, a very tight corset to stop you going out of shape. I'm going to hang you by the arms from a horizontal bar, three hours a day. I'm going to stretch you twice a week with a special machine. You'll feel better afterwards.'

As well as that, he prescribed a suitable course of treatment based on plant extracts, tonics and hormonal injections. Dubbelviz's self-assurance – his colleagues called him Double-vision because of his perspicacity – frightened Léon. He was terribly afraid of disappointing the doctor and of not being up to his expectations. So he got used to sleeping in a straitjacket with steel stays which kept him straight, itched horribly and brought him out in a rash. On top of that he had to hang from a small girder resembling a gallows and go to a laboratory to be stretched by a monstrous machine that pulled his arms and legs in four different directions, causing him atrocious pain in his thighs, knees, wrists and shoulders. He felt like a heretic being hung, drawn and quartered by a grand inquisitor. What had he done to deserve such torture? He consulted learned tomes on genetic disorders, but no pathology corresponded to his.

Unfortunately for Léon, the pain of this treatment was compounded by the further loss of an inch or so during the following week. Professor Dubbelviz was extremely annoyed and couldn't repress his anger.

'Are you doing this deliberately or what? Are you one of those patients who enjoy frustrating their doctor? If that's the case, then out with it. You only have to tell me, "Doctor, I don't want to get better," and we can get on with our lives.'

'But, doctor...'

'What happens to you is your responsibility. If you want to get better, I will make you better. If we fail, the fault will be yours.'

Solange came to her husband's aid. 'It's not his fault. He's followed your instructions to the letter, his courage and the effort he's put into it have been admirable. You're the doctor, give me back the husband I married. He wasn't tall, but he was my man. Give him a calf, a thigh, an arm transplant – and that's an order.'

Dubbelviz, strong when faced with the weak, weak when faced with the strong and intimidated by this masterful woman, broke off the triple torture of straitjacket, gallows and monstrous machine, and promised to try something different. From now on he stopped addressing Léon directly, addressing himself solely to Solange.

'I must insist on absolute discretion. If news of the case got out, your husband could be plagued by a crowd of charlatans. Give me a little time to think about it, this case is unique in the history of medical science.'

Now the whole family had been informed about the problem. The comments of Solange's mother, a tall, icy blonde, always impeccably dressed, were caustic:

'A woman should never marry beneath herself, no good can come of it. It will only pull her down. Who's to say Léon didn't lie about his height? How do you know he wasn't wearing a toupet to make himself look taller? After all, you'd never seen him undressed before your wedding night.'

Solange, hurt, reminded her mother of the short men who had achieved greatness: Julius Caesar, Napoleon...

All this speculation was cut short when the diminution stopped as suddenly as it had started. In four weeks Léon had shrunk by fifteen inches, bringing the top of his head down to the level of Solange's chest, to the epicentre of her cleavage. From now on people assumed he was her little brother, or even her big son, but all this in no way detracted from her feelings for him. On the contrary, from now on she called him My Little Man all the time to emphasise his virility while not ignoring his shrinkage. When they jived, for example, she would lift him up, swing him round in her arms and whisper things in his ear that sent him wild with delight. Léon, eyes shut, in ecstasy, would let himself be carried away to the point of unconsciousness.

Having retained the reflexes that went with his former condition, he had difficulty judging distances, walked too quickly or too slowly, bumped into the furniture and stumbled on the stairs. But he remained a man, if an abridged version, as his wife reminded him daily. Whenever he tried to skip his marital duties, complaining of a headache or an upset stomach, the tall, massive silhouette of Solange would rise up, grasp him with her long arms, wherever he was heading, wherever he was hiding, under the sink, behind the sofa, and drag him off forcibly to bed, where she would undress him from head to toe and deposit him on top of her – with the result that, a few months later, she was pregnant once more. Despite their recent troubles, the couple were thrilled.

Léon had acquired a certain celebrity of his own among his clientele. From all parts of France they came, and sometimes even from neighbouring countries, with their deafness, hoarseness, stammers and sore throats, to show him their nostrils, their vocal chords, or to get their eardrums unblocked. Flight personnel from the leading airlines consulted him regularly for ear problems. He was said to possess exceptional powers. Cases were cited where he had cured patients of the most recalcitrant conditions with just one consultation. The fact that he had reduced like a sauce on the hotplate only served to increase their confidence in his abilities, and some, believing him capable of growing and shrinking at will, called him a wizard, while others described him as a 'gnome with occult powers'.

3

The Family Grows

Léon regularly visited Professor Dubbelviz who continued to bombard him with his remorseless optimism and prescribed various detailed examinations.

'You have to help me, old chap. It takes two to treat a disease. If we don't manage it, it'll be because you're not trying. It's just too bad if your wife doesn't agree.'

He didn't treat him as an equal, as the colleague he, after all, was, but as an immature person who only needed to be told the minimum. When Léon started to go on about chromosomes, hormones and genetic engineering, he was cut short. There was no question of reciprocity between them. Each man to his own field.

Arrogant though he was, Dubbelviz was stuck. He sought the opinion of experienced colleagues, on the quiet, without revealing the identity of his patient, and they admitted they were baffled. They could understand neither how Léon had come to be compressed, nor why the compression had stopped abruptly. They asked to see him, but Dubbelviz refused. Léon was to remain his exclusive intellectual property.

He prescribed a growth hormone selected at random, a daily injection which made Léon put on twelve pounds in weight but just one inch in height, as good as nothing. Some mystery factor meant that Léon was condemned to be no more than four foot two inches tall. And his very high clubfoot heels emphasised his shortness rather than disguising it. He capitulated and wore the normal clothes and shoes for the half-pint he was. At that height there were still thousands of human beings – children, pre-teens, dwarves – with whom he could talk and socialise.

Since Léon had lost height, he was finding his son Baptiste, now one and a half, heavier to carry. He got out of breath just transferring him from his cradle to the kitchen or lifting him out of his pushchair. But he never dropped him. He would rather exert himself to the very limit than let go of him.

Does it have to be said? In this situation Léon was happy, as near as makes no difference. After all, apart from this slight handicap, he enjoyed full use of his limbs and mental faculties, and was still the husband of a ravishing wife who couldn't get enough of him and whom his friends envied. And to cap it all, he would soon be the father of two children. Even as a scale model he was still a very competent doctor, a high-density atom. All he had to do was to accustom himself to his new size while disregarding the sniggers from passers-by.

Now Solange took his hand in the street, crushing it in her palm. Despite the odd couple they had become, she loved him as much as ever and regarded his shrinkage as the equivalent of a severe attack of bronchitis, as some kind of virus that would clear up one day. She undertook some medical research of her own into this ailment and, unknown to Léon, passed the results on to Professor Dubbelviz. She saw it as her duty to protect her husband, all the more so now that he had been struck down. She boldly defied the mocking looks and put anyone who made the least disparaging remark in their place. She carried her pregnancy proudly before her, like the prow of some ship, and made sure everyone knew that Léon more than satisfied her in every respect.

She gave birth to a second child, a girl they called Betty. Solange's absolute preference was for first names that began with a 'B'. She was passionately fond of the letter that has given us beauty, baptism, beatitude, and Léon's sole desire was for what Solange wanted. Just like the first time, the birth was without problem thanks to the constitution of the mother, who seemed made to produce a whole string of whelps. Betty, taking after her mother, turned out to be a strapping baby with big blue eyes, freckles, a little snub nose, a ferocious appetite and solid, chubby arms and legs. At birth she weighed almost eleven pounds – a sixth of her father's weight – and was at least half a head taller than all the other babies in the maternity ward, where her robust physique was the admiration of the staff who had seldom seen such a sizeable infant; moreover her bawling was sufficient in itself to drown out the cries of all the other infants there.

'Good Lord,' Léon said to himself as he handed round sweets to the friends who had come to congratulate the mother, 'a few years and she'll be as tall as me. When she compares me with her friends' dads I'll really look like a featherweight.'

Two days later mother and child returned to the apartment, where Léon, who had been looking after Baptiste in the meantime, was waiting for her with a bouquet of dazzling white lilies, which was bigger than him. The birth had taken a lot out of Solange, and she asked him to support her as much as he could during the next few months and not to take on too many appointments in his surgery. He would just have to pass some of his patients on to his colleagues. But, like all children who believe they are the only child and then have to tolerate the arrival of a newcomer, Baptiste suddenly turned fractious, vomiting at the slightest excuse and throwing tantrums. It was so bad that his sister had to be put in a different room. Baptiste took every opportunity that presented itself to slip in to where the cradle was, drag the clothes off his little sister, pull her ears and pinch her. Léon gave him a good talking to, asked him to put himself in the place of a little girl who had just come into the world. What would he have said, as a tiny baby, if his mum or dad had treated him in that way? 'You shouldn't do things to others you don't want others to do to you.'

Baptiste ignored this fine sentiment completely. Irritated by the preachy tone, he started to kick his father on the shins. Since he had come down in the world, so to speak, Léon always sprang to the defence of the underdog. He knew what it was like to lose one's power and would not tolerate a person using their physical superiority to trample on someone weaker.

4

A Multi-tasking Mother Blows a Fuse

Unfortunately the nightmare started again just when he thought he was rid of it for good. One morning, two weeks after the birth of Betty, Léon found that his clothes were again too big for him and his shoes didn't fit, even though he now took a much smaller size. He rushed into the bathroom to measure himself and was horrified. During the night he'd lost four inches. Yet he'd slept like a log. Panic-stricken, he called Solange.

'It's happened again, it's happened again!' he cried, tears running down his face, setting off Betty, who also felt the need to exercise her voice and lungs, and was soon filling the house with her unbearably strident screams.

Despite her exhaustion, Solange immediately took her husband to see Professor Dubbelviz, who told him off, gave his ears an affectionate tug, pinched his cheeks until they went bright red and sent him off to Intensive Care. Solange had to hire a nanny, a home help, Josiane by name and a strapping Burgundian woman by nature, a veritable dragon with a moustache and red arms who had brought up generations of little brats and maintained quasi-military discipline. Alas, Léon's loss of height continued – he'd lost another two inches the previous evening. Greatly embarrassed, Professor Dubbelviz assured Solange there was no question of a life-threatening condition.

'Forgive me for being so open with you, Madame, but your Léon's in great shape. His heart is excellent, his musculature athletic, his liver, his kidneys, his spleen show no signs of abnormality, there is no degeneration of the bone structure, his blood count is perfect. Apart from the one minor drawback, he's built to live to be a hundred, though not at the same height.'

Dubbelviz had given his patient a code name: the Taper, for he was tapering off, melting away like a candle. Léon was shrivelling up at a steady rate. The height recorder, to which he was connected through electrodes attached to his feet and the top of his head, was bleeping all the time. Between each reduction his skin became wrinkled, like that of a frog or toad, before becoming smooth and elastic again. Léon was suffering a simultaneous contraction of all his members and organs, apart from one that we will discuss at a later point, and his loss of weight continued. Befuddled by tranquillisers, he cried as he realised his wretched state: he was smaller than he had been the previous day but bigger than he would be the next. Every day a fresh pair of pyjamas, of reduced length, was laid out on his bed; now they were going to have to draw on the supplies of the paediatric wards.

Finally the attack wore off – overnight, for no apparent reason. Just like the previous time, he had lost exactly fifteen inches, and when he left the hospital he was only three foot tall, the height of a two-year-old. For a man in the prime of his life, who had started out at five foot six, three foot isn't much, especially if he has a family to look after and loves his wife. He had lost weight and was only a little over four and a half stone. Now it was with great difficulty that he carried Baptiste, who looked like a giant spider stuck on his father, covering him from head to foot. And he was only two and a half!

Solange would feel sorry for him and say, 'Come on now,

Baptiste, carry your father on your shoulders, he's tired.'

'He's too heavy, he can walk himself. It's high time he grew up!'

The plaything of a demiurge that was enjoying itself in reducing him, Léon felt as if his identity had been amputated, like those who have lost a limb and can still feel it years later: his old body was orbiting his present body like a satellite round a planet; it was as if different doubles, duplicates of himself, had come one after the other in smaller and smaller sizes. For a long time his shadow retained its original size, an immense train attached to a little body: when it realised Léon, like a punctured balloon, was not going to stop getting smaller, it eventually disappeared altogether.

Leon's shrinkage had become accepted as part of the normal course of things, like the change from day to night. Solange did not sink into despair. She'd always been used to being a head taller than her husband – three more hardly made any difference, everything was just a matter of degree. She sometimes thought that Léon was growing smaller just to give her a surprise, not to be the same. She took his shedding of inches for eccentricity, an unusual method of seduction. Léon was like one of those little kids that never cease to astound you by their transformations. She gave him all sorts of affectionate nicknames and thought up a wealth of ingenious ideas to amuse him and put him in a good mood again.

'My little mannikin, you're just as handsome as you always were. We'll sort things out, don't you worry, nothing will stop our love.'

Léon found this consideration exasperating. 'Throw me out,' he would say, 'I'm not worthy to stay with you.'

They had to adapt the home to his new height: they fitted out every room with footstools, hassocks, ladders. Now Léon had to use a stepladder to get into the marriage-bed and could no longer pee standing up, he had to haul himself up onto the seat and do it sitting down, like a girl. The ultimate humiliation came when Solange slipped a chamber pot under the bed to spare him long treks to the lavatory during the night. For eating at the table he had a high chair that he mounted acrobatically by climbing the bars. Solange had given Baptiste, who was very precocious, a good talking-to in order to make him delete from his vocabulary all sorts of words his father might find hurtful: pygmy, runt, shrimp. Her warning had the opposite effect to the one intended. Since he didn't know those words, Baptiste learnt them off by heart and employed them with all the fervour of a neophyte.

When Léon sat down to watch the television news or a violent film on the little screen, Solange would ask him anxiously, 'Are you sure it's right for your age?' For now father and son shared almost the same interests, although Léon retained a certain moral authority: he had become the eldest of the family, the little big brother. And although he found the pastimes terribly boring and, to tell he truth, stupid, he had to join Baptiste in playing at cowboys and indians, with the electric train-set, with the toy castle. On the beach, no longer being able to play at volleyball or football with the big boys, he was reduced to building sandcastles with the rest of the small fry or catching the hermit crabs scuttling round the rock pools. He watched the same cartoons as Baptiste and, despite himself, started to prattle, to gabble on, to chortle like his son. And when the pair of them squabbled over a robot or an Action Man and made too much of a racket, Solange would stick her head round the door and shout, 'That's enough!' Solange's scolding voice was like the rumble of a basso continuo commanding immediate silence, her words whistling round

Léon's ears like bullets. If he demurred, the All-Powerful One would stride over and send him tumbling with a flick of the wrist, her blue eyes turning a greyish green. Now, when they went out for a walk, Solange put him in an outsize pram along with the other two.

'Don't take it amiss, Léon darling, but I can't keep an eye on three kids.'

She'd had three child seats installed in the back of the family car, a black 4x4 with high wheels and a large boot, and ordered them to keep their seatbelts fastened. Letting Léon sit in the front seat would have set off pointless fits of jealousy, so he had no choice but to comply. One day she automatically stuck a dummy in his mouth. He spat it out. After all, he still had his pride!

A wife and mother and a well-respected stomatologist, Solange was also an energetic woman who went running in the park three times a week. In the evenings, in a specially converted room at home, she went through intensive training sessions to work off the stress. While she was pedalling away on her exercise bike, lifting weights, working on her abdominals and gluteals, gleaming with sweat, jaws clenched, Baptiste and Léon would come and watch her through a window. They were fascinated by this creature, overwhelmed by her physical splendour. Her muscles stood out under her skin and stretched, slender and magnificent. They dreamt of being like her one day. Hypnotised by this giantess, Léon preferred to tell himself that it was she who had grown and not he who had shrunk. As he slumped, he noted how she had broadened out. So statuesque! Such fullness of figure! She was so tall that he could hardly see her face. It was like the summit of a mountain disappearing into the clouds. She displayed an impressive amount of flesh and curves. Her breasts were the size of his head, her pert bottom had rounded out into a balloon where he was afraid of getting lost. When she went to have a shower after finishing her exercises, she would bark, 'Right you kids, off to beddy-byes.' Léon would slink off to their marriage bed to the sound of his son's complaints – 'Why can you sleep with Mama? It's not fair!' – where he read articles on his condition in medical journals whilst waiting for his wife.

For Léon, embarrassing though it is to mention such a detail, had shrunk everywhere except for one ridiculously long appendage dangling between his legs. It was an encumbrance that he had to tuck away in a sort of string bag, a holder to enable him to walk without hindrance. He was bowed down under the burden of this excrescence, which made it awkward to get along. Nature had robbed him of everything apart from the organ of reproduction, the better to reduce him to that role. This virile member stood out like the outsize fins and spurs of certain prehistoric animals. Dubbelviz had noticed this anatomical detail and found it as incomprehensible as all the rest. He compared himself with his patient, imagining with disgust the coupling of the pair, Léon standing up between his wife's legs, sticking to her belly like a climber to a rock-face, clinging on to Solange's ample curves with his little hands. His disgust was only augmented by the fact that, according to the lab assistants who had analysed it, Léon's sperm motility was unparalleled: the speed of a galloping horse, gametes with unheard-of stamina.

In the evening Solange would play with Léon's extremity, not to make fun of him but almost admiringly, ascribing miraculous powers to it. The astonishing thing was the dis-proportion between that part, which belonged on a normal adult's body, and the reduced scale of the rest. Mischievously, she would pull his appendage, threatening to wrap it round his neck like a boa. There was something freakish about such a huge accessory on a pygmy. Léon, who was very shy in these matters, blushed at such liberties: he was annoyed with himself for being reduced to his private parts. He felt like crying out: what about my mind, does that not count for anything? Solange would amuse herself with his tool before employing it in the way any self-respecting wife would. Far from exhausting her, Solange's exercises increased her appetites tenfold and her overpowering strength crushed her husband's feeble protests. Lips swollen, nostrils quivering, she would coo, 'And now, my Little Bighorn, you're really going to get screwed.'

And screwed Léon certainly was, half reluctantly, half enthusiastically, in a mixture of terror and sensual delight. He complied, aware that he might perhaps be making a mistake, but it was a most pleasurable one. During these intimate moments he was haunted by absurdly vivid fears: that he was going to be sucked into her stomach, like the water going down the drain in the bathtub, and would disappear inside her, vanish without trace. The perfect crime. He had a vague suspicion that the huge rod on his pygmy frame was a dangerous abnormality.

For months Solange was delighted with it. Her miniature husband satisfied her in all things, she had no desire for a bigger one. He was docile, not much trouble, and did as he was told. She ruled over a world of gnomes, two children and an elf of a husband. What more could she ask for? Every morning, after having dropped Baptiste off at school and having left Betty at the crèche, she took Léon to his surgery. She was the one who lugged his heavy briefcase. Léon persisted in continuing with his professional activities: to stay at home would have been to give in to his ailment. His colleagues, two young housemen, his assistant and his patients all admired his determination. Léon worked at his desk on an adjustable chair at its highest setting, and he had had a fireman's ladder made with a cabin that could be raised or lowered to the height of his patients so that he could examine them. Seeing them from a new angle was amazing, he had no idea a human ear or throat could be so wide and deep. They seemed like caves, labyrinths or the leaves of palm trees and he felt as if he were looking at them magnified by binoculars. The membranes and protuberances looked larger than life-size to him. But that only made his diagnoses all the more acute since he saw before other doctors disorders that were just developing and infections that were gathering, which he would never have detected previously. Everyone was full of praise for the little doctor who performed miracles.

So all was for the best in this best of all worlds: diminished in size but not in stature, Léon persevered despite the tittle-tattle and the rumours. He forgot the stifling dungeon his body had become. But an embarrassing incident was to fix a permanent awareness of his deformity in his mind. One day Solange and he had taken the children to Euro Disney in the north-east of Paris. Amongst other attractions they had chosen was the special breakfast in Cinderella's castle. Snow White, Mary Poppins and Sleeping Beauty had all come to be photographed with Baptiste and Betty. When Cinderella's turn came, the young woman who was playing that role wrongly assumed Léon, wearing a Pluto cap, was a third child. Alerted by his stubble, as soon as she realised her mistake, she lost her cool and called him a pervert, accusing him of having made himself up in order to seduce her. Solange grabbed the hussy by the hair and forced her to apologise. The young woman burst into tears, blamed overwork and begged his forgiveness. But the damage was done. Léon was in despair. Now in the eyes of other people he embodied the grotesque combination of a roué in short trousers.

He went to see his parish priest. Like his wife, he was a devout believer and he told the priest of all his misfortunes as he sat opposite him in a chair in the presbytery. The priest who was quite old, kept his eyes fixed on the floor, as if he were afraid of looking him in the face. Léon felt as if he had some shameful mark, an illness that defiled him.

'Can you remember a sin you may have committed, my son?'

'No, Father, only venial ones, nothing serious.'

'Many venial sins can sometimes accumulate into a mortal sin.'

'There's nothing I can think of, I assure you.'

'God does not strike the just. If He is giving you this warning, it is not without reason. He is testing you because He loves you and wishes to spare you other torments.'

'I have searched through my memory, I can find nothing.'

'To sin without being aware of it is worse, doubling the fault through ignorance of its extent.'

'Truly, Father, I have looked without –'

'You cannot remember perhaps, but God records everything in his Great Book and is sending you the bill.'

'I have nothing to reproach myself with.'

'Do not be stubborn, my son. God pardons those who repent but strikes down those who persist in error.'

'But…'

'Pray, my son, ask for forgiveness. Accept, oh man of small stature, the cross the Lord has sent you.'

For nine months he also went regularly to see a psychoanalyst whose therapy consisted of alternating between sympathetic listening and aggressive listening. He let Léon speak then told him to see the positive side of things: he could have become obese, cross-eyed and sweaty. Instead of which he had chosen contraction, self-effacement. What style! A little bonsai instead of a great big baobab. How all those beanpoles that kept bashing their heads on the ceiling must envy him! Especially since he'd kept his thingy in perfect working order. Was there anything more important in life than to have a big pussy at one's beck and call? And he had the temerity to complain, to claim some inferiority complex or other? He had the gall to consult a psychoanalyst! What a namby-pamby!

Léon enjoyed being told off like that by his therapist. More than anything else he needed comforting, someone to tell him it wasn't as bad as all that. Sometimes his therapist would become morose and, in a confiding mood, almost whisper:

'You must realise, old chap, that every woman turns her husband into a child. It's the story of every marriage. She tames him, domesticates him, mothers him. At first he's My Wild Beast, then My Pet, finally My Baby.'

Then he would pull himself together, return to his role of counsellor and declare with forced conviction, 'Size doesn't matter. It's a prejudice. It's absolutely ridiculous to feel diminished just because you're just three foot tall. A person's charisma depends on his aura, not on his size. Even if you were to go down below three foot, which is still a respectable size, it wouldn't be a disaster. There's no cause for alarm either if you're only eighteen, fifteen or even nine inches tall. And below four inches size really doesn't matter at all any more.'

Oh, these stimulating assertions! They bucked Léon up no end. At the end of every session the psychiatrist would repeat, with a broad smile, 'Everything that's small is nice, everything that's big is nasty.'

But as time passed the mood of the keeper of the subconscious darkened and he became aggressive, suspecting Léon of being a shirker as far as growth was concerned and of trying to evade his responsibilities. He called him a swindler, gave him exasperated looks and made him sit on low chairs to diminish him even more. He subjected him to grotesque questions: Who did you sell your missing inches to? Have you made a pact with the devil? For how much? If you refuse to tell me the truth I'll double the fee for these sessions.

Léon was turned into a culprit summoned to appear before a tribunal, at the mercy of the whims of an exasperated judge, who one day threw him out, shouting, 'Bugger off, I've had it up to here with you. You really are nothing but a big baby!'

5

The Little Brats Seize Power

Some years passed.

Léon tried different medicines, prayer, meditation, Reiki, tai chi, acupuncture, Zen, the primal scream, neuro-linguistic programming. Nothing brought back his feeling of well-being from before the catastrophe. He was ready to convert to any religion, sect or party that would give him back his lost dimensions. Being their first child, Baptiste had always been the favourite of his father, who had watched over him, changed his nappies, cleaned him up and devoted all his skill as a doctor to his care. But now the little lad was almost as big as Léon; the boy was only five and the fact that he had caught up with him in such a short time had eroded the respect in which he used to hold his father. All he saw in him now was another boy, with wrinkles and hair already greying, who was telling him how to behave all the time. To play together with Léon was no longer enough, now he wanted to pit himself against him physically. Overflowing with energy, he would throw his father to the ground, grab him by the throat, throttle him. At school he was always getting into fights. He would push Léon just to provoke him, hit him in the stomach, take advantage of the fact that his penis trailed along the ground to squash it under his heel. Léon, not quite knowing how to respond, would get his breath back, realising that in a fair fight he might perhaps no longer have the upper hand. He also knew that a proper father would have taken the blows without flinching and happily accepted his function as his offspring's punchball.

Baptiste would have loved to have him as his best friend, to get up to all sorts of mischief together. But Léon, old-fashioned as he was, insisted on maintaining the hierarchy and giving him orders: stand up straight, shut your mouth, clear your plate, wipe your nose. But Baptiste was a match for him and quietly blew little balls of paper, hardened by saliva, at him through a straw. Betty, who could already walk, burst out laughing at the least of her brother's tricks and sided with him, the little vixen. Sometimes her brother would put a bucket of water on top of a half-open door and shout, 'Quick Daddy, quick!' Léon would come dashing along, push the door open and the bucket of water would soak him, sometimes even get stuck on his head, giving him a nasty bruise as well. The little imps split their sides. He pretended to laugh with them and, what's more, had to get the mop to wipe up the water for fear of being told off by Josiane and Solange. The presence of the nanny only added to his distress as she made no secret of her lack of respect: for in her mind a man had to be tall and strong.

He could have paid the children back in kind, could have played just as many silly practical jokes on them, but he was their father, he couldn't lower himself to their level. The truth is that he was afraid of those little savages, knee-high to a grasshopper though they were; he had shown his love by wiping their bottoms and giving them their bottles and now they were threatening him while pretending just to be playing games. The two of them were always after the cat, Furbelow, pulling its tail, running after it with a pair of scissors to cut off its whiskers, dumping it in the dustbin and putting the lid on; Léon was the only one who stood up for the poor animal and had rescued it from awkward situations several times. He regretted that he was just a doctor with soft hands and had never been interested in martial arts. Had he been a black belt in karate he would have given the snotty-nosed urchins a good hiding, a kick in the belly, a forearm blow across the nose to show them who was boss. He would have liked to handcuff the little bastards, clout them, squeeze them into a sarcophagus to stop them growing, the dirty little swine.

His wife had become his mother, his children sly and cantankerous companions. Like a coward, he went to complain to Solange: Baptiste was annoying him all the time, Betty made fun of him and they weren't nice at all.

'But Baptiste's only five, Sweetie, how could he hurt you?'

'Have you seen his size? Kids grow so quickly; we'll be living in a world of giants soon.'

'He's not doing it on purpose. He's just having fun.'

'Don't you realise? I have to protect myself against my own son! It's awful.'

'One day you'll start growing again, Léon dear, you'll take your place among us again.'

'He'll grow as well, Solange, I'll never recover the authority I used to have over him.'

Solange was losing patience. She had a household to run and couldn't spend all her time listening to them moaning one after the other.

'That's enough now. I hate cry-babies. If you don't stop you'll go to bed without your supper.'

The sole privilege Léon still possessed was to address his wife by her Christian name. And also to get into the cinema at half price while being banned from seeing films forbidden for those under twelve. He had no illusions: his mini-self enjoyed mini-rights. Overburdened with various tasks Solange, although a devoted wife, lost her temper at the slightest little thing, seeing her husband as both pitiful and deeply moving at the same time. He was grumpy and went round with a scowl on his face. He'd even forgotten how to laugh at himself. Why is God making us suffer like this, Solange wondered, what have we done wrong? One day she came across Léon and Baptiste having a set-to over a Game Boy and without hesitation gave each of them a box round the ears with the flat of her hand, her powerful arm. It left Léon dazed and almost knocked him out.

From now on, every time Baptiste had his bottom smacked, Léon was accorded the same privilege, just to make things fair. Even if he hadn't done anything wrong. This was especially the case because Baptiste knew how to get round his mother, charm her with his childish words and melodious accents. He got away with everything, he was cuter than his father, whose looks had been spoilt by his shrinkage that had given him the crumpled appearance of a Chinese Shar-Pei. Only the little black-white-and-grey cat still showed Léon the same affection, rubbing against his legs, curling up in his lap, unaffected by the changes in his body, grateful for his kindness.

Now the little husband sank into melancholy. He was ashamed of having to inflict his presence on Solange, his ridiculous appearance dashed her aspirations. He'd always had a hang-up about their disparity in height; now he could no longer help her and had constant need of her: all the drawers were too high, the plates too far away, the dishes too heavy, the cutlery too sharp. Solange, seeing the man melt away like snow in the sun, wondered whether her mother had not been right to warn her before their marriage. When friends asked her how Tom Thumb was she got angry for form's sake, but without conviction. She put these dark thoughts out of her mind, preferring not to think of the future. Léon was still her legal spouse and every evening Monsieur Minimum performed his marital duties, thus working, without wanting to, at procreation.

Eventually what had to happen happened: three years after Betty was born, Solange found she was pregnant again, albeit unintentionally. She had been sure that a man who had wasted away like that could not father a child. However, Léon, although in the process of diminution, remained terribly fertile. The family, their friends, even Josiane, were disapproving. Was she really pregnant again? Did she at least know for certain who the father was? Indignantly Solange protested her innocence. She was sorely tempted to take down the little husband's trousers in public to show everyone that some things remained of his former splendour. Léon was thunderstruck by the news. He wasn't sure he liked children any more and regarded that boisterous age-group as nothing more than a band of horrible brats and exasperating little minxes. Their whiny voices, their inane amusements and their vapid conversations got on his nerves. He quietly suggested a termination. Solange, very respectful of the Church's dogma, shut him in the cupboard for twenty-four hours on bread and water.

Baptiste and Betty were catching up with their father at astounding speed: Baptiste was already an inch or two taller. To maintain the order of generations, Solange had the high-chair raised on which Léon ate, though only from plastic plates, so that as long as the meals lasted he could still see himself as the head of the household to whom everyone listened. He would pontificate, comment on the news, regale them with his opinions on politics, society. Solange would express her admiration for the sharpness of his analyses and tell the little ones to take their father as a model. The rascals couldn't give a toss and kicked up a racket, knowing full well that physical reality would soon reassert itself.

Whenever Solange slipped away into the kitchen for a minute, Baptiste would immediately roll his eyes at his father in frightening fashion, roar and flex his biceps, growling, 'Want a taste of this, Shortarse?'

Léon was saddened by this lack of filial respect. Baptiste had become an overfed bruiser, a dirty little carnivore ready for any foul deed. Perhaps he was suffering from the complex of the eldest child who comes into direct competition with his father. Having seen him shrink before his very eyes, he imagined he was the cause of the reduction and gloried in it. Léon was his prisoner, his spoils of war, his booty. A great fan of Westerns, he would lasso his father at the end of the corridor, truss him up and roll him along to his mother's feet, declaring, 'There you are, mum, the moaning midget's all yours.'

He subjected his parent to some quiet blackmail: 'Do my homework for me, or else…' Léon obeyed, dressing his submissiveness up as concern for Baptiste's education. And he had to be sure not to make a mistake in a sum or a dictation – otherwise he was in for a good hiding. Léon would go up to him all smiles, seeking a little friendship, and his son would respond with a snarl that would have had the most bloodthirsty barbarian shitting his pants. For Léon home was no longer an oasis of tranquility but a theatre of blood, a minefield where everything was allowed. Taking pity on him, Solange grabbed the brother and sister who lisped, all innocent, 'We can have a laugh, can't we?' Léon, already their whipping boy, was now looked on as a spoilsport. His wife said to him one day, 'Stop being a scaredy-cat,' and the nickname stuck. Scaredy-cat forced a smile so as not to lose face but no longer left his room without the utmost precaution: the two little brats drove him up the wall, ambushing him, covering his medical files with blots, putting drawing pins in his slippers, vinegar in his wine, glue in his toothpaste. Their grinning mugs frightened him out of his wits. He had quietly acquired a motor-cycle helmet that he wore all the time, moving round his own apartment like a spy in enemy territory, hugging the walls.

6

The Eclipse

Léon's unease turned into pure fear when he heard that this time Solange was expecting twins: a boy and a girl curled up inside their egg, nice and warm, like two missiles in their silo. The ultrasound scan was a pure formality, they were already huge, developed, impatient. They formed words with their lips, knocked on the door of her belly, in a hurry to get out. Solange had put on over three stone, the children had nicknamed her the Whale. Unlike the first two, this pregnancy terrified Léon: it was no longer the sensuous curve of a belly swelling with life, it was a pouch loaded with lethal shells for which he would be the first target. Her skin would tear apart and the two projectiles explode in his face.

The time of delivery arrived, as it always does. Solange had her first contractions on 10 December, towards three in the morning. She took a taxi to the hospital with Léon, leaving Josiane, the fierce guardian, to keep an eye on the two children. It was an easy birth, as usual, despite the number of packages to take out. Solange's physique was ideal for bearing numerous offspring: she wouldn't have been bothered by the prospect of six or eight. She regarded fecundity as a gift from God. Léon, on the other hand, was bothered, in fact he was scared stiff. He felt out of place beside this huge woman and frightened by the medicinal odours of maternity, the interminable corridors, the implacable glare of the fluorescent lights. When they reached the delivery room the obstetrician, the nurse and the midwife, eyes red with fatigue, had yelled with one voice, 'No children in here!'

'I'm the father,' he had mumbled, turning pale.

'Who are you trying to kid?'

'No, it's true,' said Solange, 'he's the one who made me pregnant. It'd be too long to explain here. Would you see to me now, please, it's hurting a lot.'

A nurse threw Léon a white coat which was too large for him and the team started bustling round Solange.

At that very same time, Professor Daniel Dubbelviz, a martyr to insomnia, was going through the Taper's file again. He was furious: this patient was defying the laws of medical science, making a mockery of his expertise. Dubbelviz regarded his double shrinkage as a personal affront. Walking back and forth barefoot in his dressing gown, he went through the details of his case one by one, speaking out loud:

'Let's see, on the day he was married Léon was five foot six inches tall. His first child was born nine months later; a short time after Léon shrank progressively over three weeks until he'd lost fifteen inches, then his height stabilised. One year later a second child, a girl, was born. Léon lost another fifteen inches, this time in a few days. Once more his height stabilised. Three and a half years passed without any notable change. The only remarkable aspect: his penis has retained its original size, which makes it look immense, while in fact it's of normal dimensions, although perhaps a little broad and thick. What is the link between all these events? Let us try to reason it out; there must be a logic to all this, but what?'

He was rubbing his hands, tugging at his ear-lobe, a sign, in him, of great anxiety.

'Five foot six. First child, loss of fifteen inches. Leaving four foot three. Second child, loss of another fifteen inches. Leaving three foot, penis unchanged and nothing since. With each child he loses a little less than a quarter of his height, so, so…'

And, suddenly, it struck Professor Dubbelviz like a flash of lightning splitting the darkness: 'By George, could that be the link? Surely it's not possible. I'll have to go through my calculations again. But first of all I must warn them. Immediately!'

The idea seemed so important that, despite the lateness of the hour, he dialled the number of Léon's mobile at the very moment when Solange's labour had reached a critical point: the first of the twins was about to appear. Furious at this untimely call in the middle of the night – he left his mobile on in case one of his patients was trying to contact him – Léon left the group of medics and whispered, 'Who's that?'

'It's Daniel Dubbelviz, Léon. Sorry to trouble you at this hour. I've something of the utmost importance to tell you; I must speak to you immediately. Where are you? I'll grab a taxi and I'll be there right away. Wake Solange, what I have to say concerns both of you.'

'I'm with her now, in the maternity hospital, she's going to…'

'Oh no, I don't believe it! Call it off, stop it, I beg you.'

'Impossible. The contractions started three hours ago. Her waters have broken, she's in the delivery room, the babies are about to come out.'

'Stop her, block her womb, plug it with paper, rags. Barricade your wife, get it done. This baby has to stay inside its mother, d'you understand, IT MUST NOT SEE THE LIGHT OF DAY.'

'You're mad, Professor!' Léon murmured, so as not to

disturb the medical team attending to his wife.

'Chuck it all up, wife, children, work…'

'Are you going to explain to me what all this is about?'

'What it's about, Léon,' Professor Dubbelviz's voice was becoming frankly hysterical, 'It's that I have finally understood! UNDERSTOOD, Léon!'

'Understood what, Professor? Be brief, please, I can't keep talking for long.'

'I've worked out the connection between the various stages of your shrinkage.'

'It's not the right time, Professor. Let's make an appointment and you can explain it all to me.'

'No, it's now or never. Please, Léon, what I have to tell you is of the utmost urgency.'

'Be quick then, I'm distracting everyone here. They're giving me signs to switch off or go out.'

Léon slipped out of the door, gesturing to Solange, who was panting and choking, that he would be back immediately.

'Léon, my dear little Léon, I've discovered the key to all your troubles…'

'About time too, a bit late even…'

'Perhaps, but it's so complex… You've still time to save what you have left…'

'Go on.'

'IT'S YOUR CHILDREN…'

Dubbelviz was screaming, so loud that Léon had to take his mobile away from his ear: 'What do you mean, my children?'

'You mustn't have any more children. Can you hear me?'

Léon felt his legs tremble and he almost fell down. 'What are you trying to tell me?'

'Listen very carefully to what I'm going to say, Léon. With each baby that's been born you've lost fifteen inches. Why fifteen inches? I can't explain it, it's just a fact. You understand now?'

'I don't see the connection.'

'It's obvious, it was staring us in the face. These children come into the world at your expense. They live in order to erase you. You're not shrinking, you're retracting, like the handle of an umbrella or a tortoise's neck. Every time you have a child, you draw back into yourself; unfortunately you don't come back out again. You're going through an accelerated form of the renewal of the generations, the disappearance of the older for the benefit of the younger ones. What usually takes thirty or forty years takes a few weeks in your case.'

'Are you sure about this?' Léon almost fainted. He was panting, gasping for breath like a fish out of water. 'But why me?'

'I don't know. Perhaps you're the harbinger of a new kind of paternity. Perhaps in future all fathers will disappear as soon as they've impregnated the mothers, just as the female praying mantises devour the fathers of their offspring.'

'Excuse me, but that's an absurd theory. I have to go, the babies are coming out.'

'Léon,' (Dubbelviz's voice now took on a supplicatory tone) 'I beg you not to give up. You too have a right to life. Get out of the hospital, drive away, as far as you can, I'll give you money, you're my favourite patient. And then, I can tell you this now, I'm crazy about your wife, have been since the very first time I saw her. I'll explain everything to her.'

'Professor Dubbelviz, if this is a ploy to separate me from Solange, you're making a big mistake. I will never leave her.'

'Then you've had it, old chap. Goodbye, Léon, I really liked you.'

'Stop talking about me in the past tense, I'm still here.'

'Not for long, I assure you, you're going to deflate like a burst balloon.'

'You frighten me.'

'Don't worry, I'll take care of Solange, look after the children, their education. By the way…'

'…'

'Hello? Hello? Don't switch off, Léon. One last question: are you for state schools or private schools? For or against assignment to the nearest school? I will respect your wishes scrupulously. Hello?…'

At that moment the battery of Léon's mobile gave out. He dashed back into the delivery room just at the moment when the first baby, Bérénice – like a true gentleman her brother, Boris, had stepped aside to allow her out first – had just popped her head out of Solange's vagina and was using her little arms, bracing herself against her mother's thighs and buttocks, to extricate herself by her own efforts from the maternal lodgings. Léon, who had automatically sat down on the chair on which Solange had thrown her coat and handbag, was horrified by her determination, her aggressive, swaggering air. Bérénice shook herself, brushed off the mucus she was covered in with a tight-lipped look of disgust, massaged her scalp as if to reinvigorate herself and clicked her fingers for soap and a face-cloth, declining all offers of help from the hospital staff. Boris followed almost immediately with the same ease, arms stretched out, hands together, like an Olympic diver. He was caught in the safety net underneath Solange, where he bounced up and down like a ball: the maternity hospital had had some rare, very rare cases of rocket babies who shot out of the uterus and had to be caught in flight. The twins hardly cried at all, just enough to follow tradition. They were full of energy, bouncing up and down in their cot, displaying an obscene vitality.

Solange had given birth in no time at all, a mere thirty minutes at most, and the medical staff, astonished at how easily it had gone, were relaxing and preparing a toast to the young mother.

All at once Léon felt quite weak, a veil fell over his eyes and, to the alarmed looks of the nurse, the midwife and the obstetrician, he started to get smaller. Inch by inch he melted away, like a slab of butter on a stove.

'What does he think he's doing?' a nursing auxiliary stammered.

It was a long but steady reduction that lasted a good fifteen minutes, a progressive fading away before the horrified gaze of the adults. They presumed it was an optical illusion, while the twins sat up and clapped their hands, laughing their heads off at the sight. Convinced they were seeing witchcraft at work, the nurses ran off to seek help.

But Léon did not vanish into thin air, he stopped when he was four inches from the ground, the size of a pencil or a penknife. Dubbelviz had got his sums wrong: nature being good at arithmetic, the birth of the twins had only cost their father thirty inches in height, as had the two older children, plus another two inches for good measure, still leaving him enough to continue living on a small scale. It was fortunate that he had instinctively sat down on that chair when he came back from his telephone conversation. Quickly recovering his presence of mind, he took advantage of the kerfuffle to run over to Solange's coat hanging over the back of the chair and slip head first into the right-hand pocket, landing on a heap of loose change, mints, parking tickets and a set of keys attached to a little rubber cow that squeaked when you squeezed it. When Security arrived, all that could be found was a mobile on the floor broken into three pieces, the microchip crushed in all the running about. They thought they must have been victims of a collective hallucination.

Only Solange had seen and understood everything; she just cried, suggesting exhaustion and post-natal trauma. For form's sake they organised a quick search, looking for Léon in the mouse holes, loose electric sockets, ventilation shafts, then forgot the phantom father. The police opened a file on him, registering him as a missing person guilty of desertion. Thus he sank into the oblivion that is official statistics. A few patients and colleagues were sorry to lose him – his friends had long since abandoned him.

Two days later Solange was discharged from hospital with her two babbling babes in her arms and her very little husband huddled up in her coat pocket, caressing him with her fingertips to comfort him.

Part 2

Pippin The Short in all his Glory

7

Your Lowness

This time Léon had entered another dimension: he had not simply shrunk, he had moved into a different world. It was a real shock for Solange: her husband was leaving her in the lurch just when she had most need of him. Really, you couldn't count on men! She took it amiss that he had wriggled out of his responsibilities and found it difficult to believe the version of events given by Professor Dubbelviz. There she was, with four children on her hands, plus a strange creature the size of her big toe prattling on breathlessly in an inaudible babble. The sprig of humanity that she had to put her ear right next to in order to understand him kept on saying, 'It isn't my fault, I did nothing, I'm innocent.' Solange shrugged her shoulders: what was it to her that he felt sorry, the damage had been done.

Once again they had to reorganise their life together as a matter of urgency. Solange filled two trunks with her late husband's things and sent them to a charity shop. She kept a few mementos: photographs, cufflinks, silk ties, handkerchiefs. Léon was housed in a snug and fragrant cedar of Lebanon cigar box lined with dark-red velvet that she kept on her dressing table. In their days of wedded bliss the two of them used to smoke a Cohiba or a Montecristo in the evening, but Léon had had to give up the ritual, the least puff of smoke constituting a serious threat to his tiny lungs.

As far as their friends and relations were concerned, Léon

was reported missing. His surgery was taken over by one of his colleagues to whom Solange – on getting married they had opted for joint ownership of property – sold the part that belonged to Léon for a good price. That left the most important point: to see to it that nothing got out about what had really happened. Solange let Josiane, the nanny, in on the secret. She crossed herself several times when she heard of Monsieur's latest metamorphosis, but a hefty rise in wages persuaded her to swear not to breathe a word of it. The two babies couldn't speak yet, even though they seemed to have understood everything. As for the two older ones, shame sealed their lips tighter than any threats: for a long time already their father had been a source of humiliation at school and he had been ordered never to come and collect them.

Dubbelviz, who had started to court Solange persistently, would obviously hold his tongue. Strict rules were put in place: not a word about Léon in the presence of visitors. At the sound of the doorbell, the little husband was to return to his cigar-box immediately and no one was to open the door before he was shut in. If school-friends were invited for tea or a birthday party, the microbe's box was double-locked and Solange hid it in her safe. This *omertà* worked perfectly.

Anyone who infringed these simple but draconian rules left themselves open to the most severe punishment. Josiane was elected political commissar to the family, in charge of discipline with instructions to maintain order among the brood with an iron hand. Solange gave her a pliant willow cane to deal with recalcitrants: Baptiste tasted its stinging bite more often than the others. Josiane gave Léon a code name: Your Lowness. She had to exercise restraint to stop herself from spraying him like a mosquito.

'You're lucky that you're under Madame's protection,' she

kept telling him.

It was such an abrupt change for Léon that it took him a long time to realise how far it went. Nothing had prepared him for this horrendous state; he had given up trying to understand what was happening to him and had not been convinced by Dubbleviz's explanations. What a strange feeling it was to find himself the same size as his children's toys after having been as the son of his own wife. To him human beings, including his better 'half', now looked like dragons or tanks, beings in full armour, while he felt he was going naked, a tiny scrap of flesh that anything could crush. Even his love-hose had disappeared in the storm: all that was left at the bottom of his belly was an insignificant pendicle. Why had the Great Clockmaker put him out of tune with the rest of the world?

First of all there was the question of his own safety. Everything had become problematic. He avoided taking too many showers in the mug Solange had allocated him in the bathroom for fear of shrinking in the wash. You can never be too careful. Even when the tap was only turned on a little, the flow of water was like a cataract that could have swept him away in a second. To slip into the washbasin and be sucked down the plughole could be fatal. Eating was no easier: his food consisted of soups and purées; they assumed his minuscule teeth would be unable to chew even tiny bits of meat. What could a person of that size swallow? With its thick lips his mouth was so narrow that a grape, a pea and a crumb were like a banquet for him. At least they allowed him to eat with them, except for times when they had guests; now that he was half the size of a paintbrush he was put on a chair from Betty's doll's tea-party set but it was still too big for him. His food was served in a half-thimble. The thing that Léon found most horrifying was the noise of the Humans; the voices of the Immense Ones, as he called other people, shattered his eardrums, subjecting them to intolerable vibrations. Every word that came from the lips of Solange or the children was like a clap of thunder. 'Not so loud,' he would beg them, 'I'm not deaf.' When Solange spoke to him, holding him standing up in the palm of her hand and articulating distinctly, as if she were addressing a half-wit, she drenched him, without realising it, in a shower of spittle. Even the briefest conversation required a hat, oilskins and umbrella.

He had been naïve enough to imagine he would no longer have anything to fear from his children. In their eyes Léon had ceased to be a rival or a source of shame and had turned into an anatomical oddity: an animated toy; as for himself, he had never before thought them so monstrous and ugly. The two babies bawled all day long and the little devils' horrible cries went right through him. As for the two older ones, it was even worse. Have you ever been present while two kids are having lunch? These little cherubs with their jaws working overtime, their little pink tongues popping in and out, have charms that would bring tears to the eyes of the most hardened criminal. But when you're no bigger than a pea-pod those vicious mandibles, those sharp fangs, those glistening lips, those chubby fingers the size of hammer beams are swords, clubs, fiery furnaces ready to swallow you whole, to tear you apart. They dribble, they spit, they burp in the most disgusting manner. You're at the mercy of two little gluttons unaware of their own power.

And when one of them let out a fart in his presence, he would almost faint. These pink-faced little rogues with the clear, shining eyes found it difficult to imagine that this rubber puppet that twisted and turned every which way could at some point have been their father. Their interest was now focused on

Daniel Dubbelviz, who came every day in the late afternoon to pay his respects to their mother and showed a strange deference towards the homunculus. Solange would greet him politely but not effusively. Clearly there was no place in her heart for him, her grief had closed it up.

One word had disappeared from the family's vocabulary: Daddy. They nicknamed Léon the Midge and, as if that were still too fine for him, they called him the Louse. However, Léon had not given up; he wanted to prove to Solange that he was still capable of carrying out his duties as head of the family. One evening he decided to take charge of supervising dinner himself. Standing between the salt cellar and the water jug, he bawled out orders, stamped on the table, uttered threats. Baptiste, reverting to his former attitude, grasped him round the waist and lifted him up until he was level with his eyes, to the cheers of his sister and the squeals of the twins stretched out in their Maxi Cosis.

Léon screamed at the top of his voice, 'Put me down, Baptiste. That's an order and I won't tell you twice.'

Solange had just left the table to go and heat up bottles for the twins. With a flick of his fingers, Baptiste sent his little father flying head first into a bowl of purée, fortunately warm, in which Léon nearly suffocated. Solange, who had come back into the room in the meantime, merely directed a 'tut, tut' at the little brat, wiped Léon down with a Kleenex and sent him off to bed in his cigar-box without a word.

The attempt had failed.

In their indifference towards him the children were capable of playing nasty tricks on him, which were exacerbated by thoughtlessness. One day Baptiste, calling his father 'my little soldier', dipped him head first into a boiled egg that had been opened for some time, where Solange found him stuck, feet in

the air, beating time. Once more the little devils were making
his blood run cold: from the moment they woke they were
croaking like frogs, pulling each other's hair, pinching each
other's toys. Little savages. Baptiste, the stronger, would give
his sister a real thrashing and she would cry blue murder; in
return he got a good hiding from Josiane. He was so tough
he hardly cried. The two monsters would then make up by
terrorising Boris and Bérénice with grimaces and wild howls.
Léon was still afraid of becoming the target of their over-
excited nerves; he knew that in some beings frailty could
arouse murderous instincts. He sensed that they were close to
squeezing him between their thumb and index finger just to see
what would happen. He would have loved to convert them to
non-violence, to instil a little moderation into them, convince
them that harmony was better than discord, but how? How
could he exercise any authority at all when he looked like a
hairpin? He had spent fifteen years acquiring his qualifications,
living on scholarships and grants, and look where it had got
him! At night the tiny father had horrible nightmares: his
children stabbed him with forks, carried his head on the top of
a fountain pen, chopped him into little pieces in an automatic
pencil sharpener or pulled him apart, limb by limb, like a
dragonfly, a grasshopper.

How could one blame them? In their eyes he wasn't a
human being but a corpuscle. He bore no grudge against Betty
(now five) for having popped him in the toaster while it was
switched on; fortunately he'd been able to jump back up from
a slice of bread that was being toasted but he'd scorched his
calves and choked at the infernal heat of the machine. Nor
against Baptiste (almost seven) who had tied him by the foot
to a piece of elastic to bounce him up and down like a yoyo
until he brought up his dinner (veal chops in calvados sauce

and gratin dauphinois). Nor against Boris (six months) for having put him in his mouth – Léon had managed to jump out before his jaws closed on him. They were children, they didn't know what they were doing. But in the evening, when he was back in his cigar box, his curfew having been set at eight o'clock, he had plenty to worry about. The Shrimp became taciturn. He thought back to all those summers on the beach, their occasional skiing holidays, the little bistros where he and Solange had enjoyed chilled white wine, scalding espressos. Their carefree days, their happiness had only lasted a few years. He had hardy tasted the good things in life. His body was as cramped as a coffin.

He was wary of everyone and everything. He had added the cat to his list of potential enemies. In his imagination the adorable Furbelow, that he had so often saved from being tormented by the children, had turned into a tiger chasing him round the house with throaty growls. He was sure she wanted to eat him raw, but not without having tortured him first, so there was no point in reminding her of their former feelings of friendship and respect. He could already see her climbing up onto Solange's dressing table, watching him as he hid underneath her powder compact, or behind a jar of cream, or a lipstick, and pouncing on him, knocking him to the ground with a blow of her graceful paw armed with five sharp daggers, each pad the size of a pillow.

When Léon wanted to get out of his box he would cautiously lift the lid a little, convinced that Furbelow, crouching in ambush, was only waiting for that moment to drag him out with her claws stuck into his tender flesh. He would try all sorts of ploys, and, as if he were on a battlefield, he would throw out decoys – a doll's sock, a pair of trousers – then wait and try again. He thought the animal capable of spending hours without moving, without breathing, completely in the grip of its predatory urge.

As a precaution he pinched an orange-stick from Solange's manicure set and sharpened it to a point so that he could use it as a spear in case of attack. He was a warrior now and had to go about armed.

Léon was wrong in this but he would only learn that later. Furbelow was the only one in the household who never betrayed him.

8

Winning Back Hearts

After several weeks Léon's prison-like regime eased
somewhat: his timetable became more flexible, discipline was
relaxed. Solange, despite everything she had on her plate, was
once more the caring wife she had been. She had searched
on the Internet, discreetly questioned her friends: the cases of
husbands who had shrunk until they were a wisp of straw were
extremely rare. There was no allusion to them either in the Old
or the New Testament. For her there was absolutely no doubt
at all: God was testing her faith. Recalling her marriage vows,
she promised Léon she would never abandon him and would
look after him as the only man she had ever loved. Explaining
to him that they could no longer sleep together, she moved
him out of the cigar box and installed him in a six foot by
nine boxroom right at the rear of the apartment, close to the
back stairs, at the end of an interminable winding corridor,
where they stored brooms, suitcases, cardboard boxes, cast-off
clothing and other discarded items. Solange adored corridors,
comparing them to long rivers that connect different countries.
In this cubbyhole she got a carpenter to make a shelf five feet
above the floor, out of reach of the kids and the cat, on which
she fixed a hamster house, spick and span with a door at the
front. This 'chalet' was placed on a teak floor surrounded by
a solid balustrade on which Léon could put out his washing
to dry. He did all his housework himself, having learnt to

do sewing and ironing in the orphanage where he had been brought up.

Léon couldn't understand why his wife didn't want to sleep with him any longer. It wasn't as if he weighed twenty stone and might break the conjugal bed with his weight. He hardly took up the space of a mug. Exactly! Solange said, I could roll over on you by accident, throw you in the waste-bin without noticing. Since he had to move he would have preferred to go to the lovely doll's house Betty had been given the previous Christmas and live in the first-floor room with the four-poster bed, the old-style bathroom with chrome taps, a wide terrace and a rocking chair where he could read in the sun. His daughter had refused point-blank, threatening to smash the lot if the 'thing' should go to live there.

His high-rise apartment had the look of a cuckoo clock which he reached by means of a lift in the shape of a salt cellar powered by an electric motor. (Solange had bought it in a toy shop specialising in construction sets.) A toboggan on a kind of helter-skelter allowed him to slide back down. It was all ingenious but fragile, especially since both the children and the cat never tired of playing with the wires of the lift until one day Furbelow, by accident, sliced through the main cable, wrecking the whole system. At least Léon hadn't been in the lift at the time. Solange, with the patience of Job, then gave him a little plastic spiral staircase with banisters either side and seven landings with panoramic views where he could rest, as well as a knotted string to pull himself up by. That gave him some exercise and after a while he made a game of it, going up the steps two by two while timing himself, climbing up and down the string until his palms were covered in calluses and his biceps bulged.

Other day-to-day problems had to be sorted out. As we

have already said, it was no use Léon shouting himself hoarse, no one could hear him. A bizarre midget with a falsetto voice, he was forced to scream until his voice gave out when trying to make himself heard. His vocal cords were not powerful enough. He made himself a kind of megaphone out of half an empty ink cartridge and half a Metro ticket and spoke through it. But the device was heavy to carry, cumbersome and not very effective. A telephone was out of the question, the old-style receiver was ten times Léon's own weight and even the new version of the latest model of mobile was the size of an articulated lorry in relation to him. Fully dressed, Léon now weighed ten ounces. It was impossible for him to call for help during the night if he was ill or if Furbelow should launch a surprise attack. Solange gave him a little bell, that had been round the neck of a doll, for him to warn her in case of danger. As her bedroom was over twenty feet from Léon's lumber room, as good as light years away, it was unlikely she would ever hear it, even if he were ringing it frantically. He had lost the right to fall ill during the night.

All these trials and tribulations gave Léon renewed energy. They were almost a relief – he could fall no lower. No longer able to father any more children, he would stop shrinking. A certain confidence returned and he decided to fight, to face up to the world with increased boldness. He still had a role to play. To start with, he told Solange he wanted to read the papers in the morning. She spread the dailies and magazines out on the boxroom floor; he sat down some distance away, usually on the first landing of his staircase, with a pair of binoculars and found out what was in the news. He went down to turn the pages over himself; it was difficult if a draught or a puff of wind came as he was doing it and more than once he had found himself wrapped up in newspaper, like a fillet of whiting. He also listened to the radio, but from a good distance away, and watched television with a telescope, so huge the screen seemed to him. This positive attitude bore fruit. Charming and tactful towards Solange, he let her go out in the evening to be wooed by Dubbelviz and bent over backwards to relieve her of her burdens. As mistress of the house exhausted by having had too many children, she found great comfort in her husband's perfect manners. Living with Léon was like being married to a matchstick, but a loquacious, amusing and touching matchstick, a shrill little chatterbox with a ready tongue.

It was almost the start of a second, clandestine honeymoon for them, if that word isn't going too far for a couple of such staggering disparity. The giantess scrutinised her jumping bean through a magnifying glass. He was so cute and perfectly proportioned – pity it was impracticable. She got into the habit of taking him with her when she did the shopping, a stowaway in her pocket or handbag. At home Léon would talk to Solange, perched in her ear, his hands cupped round his mouth. Outside the two were linked by a miniature radio system, on the lines of the tiny earphones used by television presenters. When they were at the market together Léon gave his wife advice from the smell, telling her how ripe the peaches, nectarines and melons were, indicating which produce to buy with the aid of a spyhole in her jacket. As far as clothes were concerned she would go to the doll's section in the supermarket for his trousers, jackets and cardigans; usually they had to be taken in, so that most of the time he wore girl's clothes, but what did that matter, given his state? When they went to a fair with the children, she would allow him little treats, feeding him a few strands of candyfloss or a piece of bright-red toffee apple. Clinging to her side, like an insect on an elephant's skin, rocked by the rhythm of her steps, warmed by her body-heat, Léon was as happy as a sand-boy. These pleasures made up for his previous trials and tribulations. He was no longer just Solange's husband but part and parcel of her ample body.

He had a terrible fright one day: a thief snatched Solange's handbag when she put it on the shop counter to pay for her purchase, and ran off down the street, shouldering other people out of the way. Sure that he'd thrown off his pursuers, the thief stuck his finger into the bag to get the purse. Léon gave it a vicious bite. Imagining it was a snake or a rat, the man dropped the bag and ran off. This act of bravery made Léon the family hero – for a week – and led to a lasting rapprochement between husband and wife, much to Dubbelviz's displeasure. In the evening Solange would tell him her worries: pressure of work in the practice, bad-tempered or over-sensitive patients, registering the twins for the nursery school, Baptiste's problems – hyperactive and violent at school, poor marks compared with his sister, who was already more settled and hard-working. Léon soothed her anxieties, was generous with advice and offered to coach his son.

Solange let him participate secretly in almost all aspects of her social life. She had gone back to wearing stiletto heels, now that her husband was so short it made no difference. When his statuesque wife, stretched out on her sofa in a lace bodice and fishnet stockings, entertained friends on Sunday afternoons – when she kept open house – to him she seemed as magnificent as an idol, as majestic as a queen. He had become her *éminence grise*, snuggled up in one of her pockets or the cup of her bra. He was the sovereign Dwarf before whom all these giants bowed, without being aware of it. He remained the master of ceremonies who organised the musical programme in the afternoons (soft jazz, blues, opera). Her visitors were colleagues from work, cousins, admirers, all of whom commiserated with her, having got wind of the awful disappearance of her husband. Recently widowed, she was much courted by suitors. Léon did not take umbrage at this, indeed it gave him a certain pride. After all, these tributes reflected on him and Solange showed such skill in keeping these men dangling, playing them off one against the other, starting with Dubbelviz, the first on the list, that he quivered with delight. He took part in the conversation, whispering cutting or malicious retorts to his wife. Solange would give little shrieks in a shrill voice that contrasted with her size and have fits of the giggles, like a little girl, that melted the hearts of the company.

Sometimes one of her guests, under the guise of expressing his sympathy for his hostess, felt obliged to make some catty remark about Léon and the disaster he'd been; it was marvellous then to hear Solange put him in his place for his tactlessness and forbid him to insult her late husband in her house. Those who ventured to do this once, first and foremost his mother-in-law, never repeated their mistake.

Dubbelviz was the leading figure in the band of admirers. He had his chair, in which he stretched out his long legs, smoked big cigars, drank his beer, took the children on his knees to play and made a great fuss of them. Léon felt a twinge of regret: his situation was like that of a dead man returning to the scene of his previous existence and finding his place taken. He was also aware that one day Solange would have to make a fresh start in life and that Dubbelviz, who for years had been passionately in love with her and very attentive to her every need, remained the best candidate, even if he evoked no response in her. It would be a marriage of convenience, not of passion. The very idea made him feel sick, but Léon had no choice. All in all, he preferred to control her remarriage, if it had to happen, rather than be its victim. He would remain Solange's sole love, of that he was sure, the father of her children, struck down in his prime by mysterious circumstances. Dubbelviz, realising that his matrimonial chances depended on the goodwill of his former patient, showed Léon respect inversely proportional to his abbreviated stature. He was constantly flattering him, his favourite approach being:

'Léon, you're a stage in the development of mankind: a demonstration of the possibility of life on a small scale in an overpopulated world. You're a mutant, Léon, you're showing the way forward for the species.'

It was wonderful to see this giant – he was well over six feet tall – bow before the Pipsqueak and consult him. In fact, like Josiane, Dubbelviz was slightly afraid of Léon, seeing him as all the more dangerous because he seemed so insignificant. He would have preferred to see him disappear for good and was racked with jealousy at Solange's rapport with her husband.

9

Formula 1

When she was alone with Léon, Solange showed him little attentions that he found deeply moving; for example, when she had a cup of tea she would put a cup for him on the tray, as if he were still able to drink with her. She would fill it, add a drop of milk and sugar it the way he used to like it and let it slowly cool without touching it. One evening, when they were alone together on the sofa watching television, he on her knee, she in a skirt and no tights, Solange fell asleep. He had leant down and seen, at the end of an interminable avenue of smooth, tanned flesh, the swell of her white panties like a sail billowing in the wind. Blown away by the beauty of this panorama, this immense screen concealing all the glories of existence, he had fallen onto the floor and bumped his head. But he had no regrets at having looked.

Solange did her utmost to make his life easier. She constructed things to match his size and had given him a doll's watch, the dial of which only he could see, made with finely toothed wheels that chipped away furiously at the hours and minutes. As a first sign that he was back in favour she had made him a tub out of a silver box placed on a little varnished table in the bathroom. He would sit down on a pearl from her necklace, beside her jewellery box, and admire her. He stared, open-mouthed, at the little knobbles of her spine which he would have loved to climb, step by step, like a tree that would take him up to heaven. Husband and wife would have their baths together and Léon would watch his gigantic spouse, her body covered in soap, rub herself with her long hands until she told him off and asked him to turn round. With just one squeeze of her shiny pink nails she could have severed his wrist or even sliced off his head, and this simple fact only served to increase his admiration for her.

She did have her absent-minded moments: she would leave him in fitting rooms or on taxi seats; she would put him somewhere – in her dressing-gown pocket, on the edge of the sink – and forget him. He would wait in a mixture of mild irritation and amusement. She would automatically put him away in the drawer with the corkscrew, throw him into the waste-paper basket along with the opened envelopes and she would then spend whole nights looking for him with her torch. He was the size of her finger and she sometimes used him to scratch her back without realising it was her husband. He imagined a future as a tooth-pick or a cotton bud in the world of the Biggies.

It was during this period that she gave him a fantastic present for getting round the house: a 1940s Jaguar drop-head coupé, a lovely cobalt-blue car, valveless, mahogany dashboard, two brass radiators, chrome grille, wire wheels and an average speed of seven miles per hour, touching ten on a straight. It ran on electricity, not petrol, so it just had to be recharged overnight by plugging it into the mains like a mobile. It had been difficult for Léon always having to depend on others to get round the flat. There were miles of corridor between his own quarters and the communal rooms – it took him ten minutes each morning to get to breakfast, which meant he had to get up well before the others if he wanted to participate in the collective ritual. If he was late, the gang would have dispersed, the children already off to school and Solange to the dental practice. He would be left all alone with the remains of a finished meal: soggy cereal in the bottom of a bowl, the butter soft, the jars of jam opened, slices of toast half-eaten and abandoned, dirty knives, with the smell of cold coffee hanging over the shambles. And the nanny, as welcoming as a prison guard, would whisper, as she picked him up by the collar like a kitten she was about to drown, 'Is Your Lowness taking tea or coffee this morning? A crumb of bread, a drop of orange juice, a bit of muesli? You have to eat your muesli if you want to grow up to be a big boy…'

Her particular pleasure was to chase him with the vacuum cleaner and gobble him up like a piece of fluff in the bellowing maw of the machine. Every time she claimed she hadn't seen him, pretended she'd been clumsy, was surprised. Privately she would encourage Furbelow to go ahead and gobble up its master if he should come within reach of its jaws and the children knew she would forgive them if they should happen accidentally to catch him with their clodhoppers.

He had to learn how to drive again and retake his licence for miniature cars. The chances of an accident, even in a nineteenth-century Parisian apartment, were numerous, especially as he had no seat belt: if, for example, he should take the folds in the carpet at too sharp an angle, he could overturn, tip over backwards. Freshly waxed wooden floors were as dangerous as a road with black ice. Certain gaps, where the floorboards had warped, were veritable potholes. On the old-fashioned kitchen tiles he could go into a spin on any patch of grease or drop of oil that happened to be there. And driving on the thick fitted carpet was an art in itself: he had to keep going at a steady speed to stop the car getting stuck in the pile. If that did happen, Léon had to sound the horn, to summon help, hoping that surly Josiane would come to his aid before the ravening Furbelow skidded to a halt before him, licking its chops. Fortunately the Jaguar was fitted with an alarm, half foghorn, half fire siren, that the cat was still afraid of.

Despite all the perils driving the car involved, how much there was to enjoy! Oh, the route along the corridor to the sitting room with its two right angles: it was like entering a steep-sided canyon with two lethal bends before a long curve took him into the hall. He would rev up noisily, put on his leather helmet and goggles, switch on the headlights and set off, foot right down, doing controlled skids to the roar of the Jaguar's 1000 hp. The aristocratic Jaguar, heedless of obstacles, would sometimes graze one of the walls, sending it across to the other side, swaying and swerving dangerously, and Léon would take his foot off the pedal before putting it down again hard. What the hell! And the tyre burns he left behind him! He wore out the tyres in a few weeks. At certain times of the day he would take advantage of the fact that everyone was out to time himself on marathon drives round the flat. From the front to the back door via the sitting room in less than five and a half minutes – better that! He drove with his hand on the horn and his foot right down, going through red lights, in the wrong direction down one-way streets and mounting the pavement – so what?! He saw Furbelow in the distance, the cat's coat bristling at the noise, scampering off at top speed, tail fluffed up, fur standing on end, to escape the speeding car. As he whizzed past, Léon gave the cat the one-finger salute: 'Fuck you, pussy!'

He also hoped to impress Baptiste with his exploits. Part of Solange's authority had devolved upon him since, as the eldest, he was the only one who could assist her. Baptiste was irritated by the affection still shown by his mother, brothers and sisters to Léon, who had become one toy amongst others. He mounted an untiring propaganda campaign against him, pointing out that his luxury car had cost a fortune – which came from the sum allocated for their own games. Their father, although one tenth of their size, was in receipt of the better part of the household budget: an ebony bed, silver bathtub, millionaire's wheels, linen, silk and cashmere clothes, and costly delicacies. It was just so unfair, there had to be an end to this favouritism. He urged Betty to join him in his revolt against this iniquity and to stop the little squirt making their lives a misery by whizzing round the corridors in his backfiring old banger. The pair of them even managed to set the twins, hardly a year old, against their father.

It was the beginning of a guerilla war. Harassed in his activities as a racing driver, Léon had to do an emergency stop and pull over whenever he encountered one of his kids for fear of being crushed underfoot like a peppercorn. His children were incapable of strolling or even of walking normally. They had only one mode of locomotion: a stampede. One day when Baptiste was haring along at full tilt, having pinched one of his sister's favourite dolls, he slipped on a marble close to Léon, who was driving, bare-headed and whistling to himself, with an American cigarette between his lips. The sole of Baptiste's right shoe struck the Jaguar, sending Léon shooting out of the vehicle like a champagne cork and it was mere chance that he wasn't completely crushed. The bonnet of the car was crumpled, the bodywork smashed, the main shaft twisted, the dashboard ripped off. Holding his hand over his mouth to conceal his giggles, the lad hardly apologised and, seeing his sister bearing down on him to get her doll back, ran off again uttering wild cries.

It was never established whether it was an accident or a

deliberate act of sabotage. But Solange was furious. Any anarchy in her realm would send her into a rage. With her the expression 'to look daggers' took on its full meaning: her eyes narrowed, fixing a steely-sharp gaze on the culprit. No one was proof against its piercing power and the glare was always the prelude to an explosion. And indeed, she began to vent her wrath: her fury made the walls tremble, the chandeliers quiver. It was like the din of a cannonade, of a squadron of bombers passing overhead. For good measure she decided to punish the whole household, even the cat was put in a corner and tied to a radiator by its tail, even Dubbelviz, who was deprived of his visits for a whole week, even Josiane, whom she accused of laxness, grabbing her by the collar and shaking her vigorously. The nanny, although humiliated by this, promised to support her better and to apply the rules with a severity that would make children and grown-ups toe the line. Solange sent everyone to their room, including Léon, who was confined to his eyrie and forbidden to come back down until further notice. The kids, who, despite everything, were sorry at the destruction of the beautiful machine, kept their heads down until the storm had passed. Solange called an extraordinary general meeting and announced that she would not be buying another since the Jaguar had already been too expensive. Baptiste, full of feigned contrition, rubbed his hands, having deprived his brat of a father of all means of transport.

10

An Over-inquisitive Husband

Léon forgave his offspring everything and still hoped to regain
their respect. He refused to be demoralised by the situation
in which he found himself; despite the loss of his luxury car,
his enthusiasm was undimmed. Especially since Solange had
secretly promised to get him a new vehicle soon; not necessarily
another car, it was to be a surprise she would give him once the
young fry had calmed down. She had to apportion her largesse
equitably, to avoid encouraging rebellion.

To make up for this, as a special treat she allowed her Tom
Thumb to sleep in her pyjama pocket, above her heart, an
exceptional privilege she kept from Dubbelviz. Léon didn't
need to be asked twice. He had found being banished from
the marriage bed very hard and was overjoyed to be able
to return to its immense canopy which was like the Milky
Way, with its immaculate white sheets, and its soft, swelling
pillows which he could slide down as if on sand dunes. Before
going to sleep, Solange would hitch up her pyjama jacket and
ask him to perform some little services for her: varnish her
fingernails and toenails, push back the cuticles with a piece of
wood, rub a numb finger back to life, scratch her back with a
big-toothed comb, massage her spine and knead her stomach
while squeezing the folds.

Solange's skin was a vertiginous chessboard with freckles
the size of coins, lozenge shapes separated by grooves, almost

channels, some deeper, some less deep, Léon crossed with a standing jump. After he had given her body a thorough working-over, she would examine him, her eyes puffy with sleep, and sigh, 'What a good-looking lad you are, Léon dear. If only you were a few inches bigger.' Then she immediately fell asleep.

That was the tricky moment. Before she lay still, her body quivered and jerked. Her tongue made smacking noises, she turned to the right and left to find a comfortable position, pulled the blankets snugly round her and didn't sink into a deep sleep before having discharged a salvo of snores like the rumble of thunder. Léon only had a few minutes to get back to his cotton berth. He would curl up there and close his eyes, rocked by the cushion of flesh with its sweet, milky smell, rising and falling like the swell of the sea. Sometimes, in a burst of affection in the middle of the night, she would press him to her bosom, almost suffocating him, and he came to feel he would like to die in that passionate embrace. In the morning Solange, not wanting to wake her mini-husband, would hang up her pyjama jacket on a coat-peg, telling Josiane to go and collect her husband when he indicated that he wanted to get up. She had bought him a police whistle so that he could let people know where he was in the apartment. But the nanny, claiming to be hard of hearing, never heard him, and Léon could stay hanging up there until the evening, his lips dry from all the whistling.

After a few weeks he had become the official warden of Solange's body, the recorder of her interior climate, the grand chamberlain of her temper and temperatures. His nights became more restless: sleeping with his lawful wife once more he was keen to recover his conjugal rights. He would open his eyes around two or three o'clock in the morning, climb out of his pocket and, equipped with a head-torch he had fabricated from parts of Baptiste's electric train (he'd taken two headlamps off a diesel engine), start to explore his wife's huge organism that for him had become an unknown country of vast proportions. Solange, exhausted by her double existence as mother and dentist, was a heavy sleeper. Nothing could wake her once she'd closed her beautiful blue-green eyes. Léon would go round what he regarded as his property: 'All this belongs to me! Wow, am I rich!' He was fascinated by her corpulency. He would climb up towards her face, cross the long plain separating the heights of her breasts from the bottom of her neck and pull himself up, thanks to a few judiciously placed folds of skin, onto the promontory of her chin, where he would sit cross-legged just below her mouth. Then he would sweep the beam of his torch over the landscape, like a tourist sitting at the foot of a pyramid. How beautiful this woman was!

He admired the smooth surfaces of her skin, smeared with a delightful regenerating cream, the shining curves of her full, rounded lips, lips that he had so often kissed and that could now easily swallow him whole. He was intrigued by the vertical grooves, wondering if a skin sculptor had carved them with a minuscule graver when she was an infant, incising them in an unknown alphabet with the story of her future life. He stood up and ran the tips of his fingers lightly over them, marvelling at their elasticity, their velvety smoothness.

He'd had to shrink before he could see his wife as a different person, more magnificent even than before his metamorphosis. As she developed, Solange had grown more beautiful. A puff of perfumed air came from her half-open lips and he inhaled the breath laden with all her bodily emanations like a gust of energy. He admired her huge eyeballs, globes of skin and flesh, the curtain of her eyelids, creased like rice paper and streaked with blue lines, that quivered according to the phases of her sleep. He would have liked to huddle behind those curtains, wash in the bitter water of her tears, lie down in the wrinkles at the corners of her eyes. He felt that if he stared at her intently he would be able to see the images of her dreams go past and share them with her. Her long black lashes, letting the light filter through like parasols, and her capacious nostrils, two deep caves blocked by thick black lianas that vibrated at each exhalation like the strings of an instrument, both filled him with astonishment. *La Serenissima* hummed, buzzed, chirped a song without words, sending out jaunty little tunes, stirring melodies that he would have liked to record. He revered these attributes like the qualities of an idol, no longer doubting that there was something divine about Solange, a being who had come down from Heaven and whose worshipper he would remain. He would have liked to scale the ridge of her nose, reach the foot of her temples, extend his exploration to her forehead, venture into her auburn hair, that fragrant forest kept in order by a headband (some had escaped in playful, perfumed locks recalling the mane of a lion) but he was afraid of waking her by trampling on her with his little feet.

If, at that moment, Solange had abruptly sat up Léon would have been swept away like a crumb, catapulted onto the bedclothes. He felt like an ant crawling up a sequoia, but he didn't care and boldly faced the dangers of his recklessness. His wife's features were perfect, arranged in absolute symmetry. Examining them was like contemplating the façade of a Gothic cathedral or a Renaissance palace, it meant going into ecstasies at both the harmony of the whole and the beauty of the details. Hanging above him, like a magnified moon in the sky, Solange's face shone with a brightness that filled him with fear and rapture. Sublime, she was sublime.

With time, he grew bolder, ignoring his wife's injunction: she had forbidden him to go you know where and had asked him not to sleep naked in order to avoid temptation. One evening he hid a length of nylon cord in his pyjamas and attached it to his wife's left nipple, a hunk of flesh the size of his leg, grainy like a rocky spur, that hardened in the cold. Thus he made his descent, passed beneath the huge breast (38E) – a cupola, a dome gleaming in the dark – leaving the grille of the ribs, where he could hear her heart beating like a big bass drum on his left. He crossed the gulf of the oesophagus to bivouac in the rim of the belly button, wide as the crater of a volcano and moulded in a complex design, a double helix left by the severance of the umbilical cord. Inside this wide-mouthed basin he could hear rumblings and gurglings. Beneath that air-filled mattress it sounded like the convulsions of blocked pipes.

Solange was digesting, fortifying her immense frame. In a few hours her stomach, empty once more, would be sputtering again, complaining it was starving. Three pregnancies had not spoilt her physique, merely emphasised that fullness of figure that took Léon's breath away. Solange's body had lived and given life and that was what made it beautiful. Léon enjoyed the sensation as her stomach rose and fell, and sometimes he would fall asleep, despite his good intentions, so that as dawn broke he had to haul himself back up, detach his cord and jump back into her pocket. And then, what if Solange, wakened by an urgent need, should get up to find a little spider dangling from her left breast? He'd be in for a real tongue-lashing, that was for sure. Sometimes Mini-man would showboat, sliding down Her Immensity at top speed, going as far as the soft swell of her hips, where there were enough love handles for a hundred Léons, rolling over and over on that well-padded

trampoline, on his plump lady love. He never ventured below
her navel, where the dry zone of thick growth begins: that
territory, barred by the frontier of a little pair of panties (white
satin, size 16), was closed to him. He had forfeited access with
his change in size. He was no longer Solange's husband but the
temporary tenant of her sumptuous anatomy. Living on that
woman was like living in a harem with a thousand different
women condensed into one. Appropriating a few fragments
wouldn't make him a burglar.

One evening, however, or rather one night with a full moon
when he had become intoxicated through inhaling more of the
heady perfume from Solange's armpits than was sensible, he
dared. He had a double length of cord with him in order to
increase his range and set out from her navel on the descent
of the stomach towards the legs. As a precaution he'd decided
to crawl, like a trapper hunting bison. The vegetation grew
more abundant, grasses tickled his nose, causing him to sneeze
twice. He knew that this path to paradise was fraught with
danger but felt strangely exhilarated at the idea of breaking
the taboo. He lifted the elastic of her panties very cautiously,
as one would move a strand of barbed wire out of the way, and
entered an area of dense undergrowth covering a large mound,
a real hillock. The lawn had obviously not been mown for a
long time. To think that in the past his wife used to remove all
body hair so immaculately that he begged her to leave a few
hairs under her arms! He took his bearings, checking with his
compass and sextant to make sure he hadn't gone astray, on the
wrong side, for example, towards her posterior, which would
have been annoying. He stretched out in the meadow, face to
the ground, sucking in the odours of the grasses: vegetable
smells mingling with the fragrance of musk-scented soap. But
another, headier aroma came up from the subsoil, redolent of

kelp and iodine, the trickle of salt water. A whole undersea world was at work beneath that promontory. It seemed as if he could hear the roar of the waves on the rocks and feel a powerful swell. He was assailed by memories of delirious happiness that went to his head and he started giving little cries, losing all restraint. Burying his head in the undergrowth, he almost felt like laughing, crying. Oh my God, if he were to go back there! Yes, why ever not? Why should he not make his home inside Solange, live in her vast apartments? Why should he not make his way back to the pocket via tunnels and pipes, slowly petrify there like a thinking fossil? No one would suspect it, not even Solange herself, he'd have board and lodging – and laundry – free, gratis and for nothing, and an end to all his worries. Eternal bliss, heaven on earth!

So there he was, stretched out on the upper ridge of the Mound of Venus, all ready to let himself slip down along the Sacred Abyss. Solange mostly slept on her back and in her sleep she had opened her legs a little. Léon looked into the chasm, completely dazzled by the view. He couldn't get over the majesty of the landscape and was looking for the easiest way down. So what happened? How did he, such a great expert on the region that he had explored so many times, allow himself to be taken by surprise? Just a little ordinary detail. His movements tickled Solange, who put her hand down to her stomach to scratch herself and, without realising it, sent her little husband tumbling down into the chasm. Her big fingers landed on him and flicked him away. Before he knew what was happening, he was plunging down, head first, felt a gust of hot air and slipped, unhurt, through a luxuriant jungle, until the two rolls of fat at the bottom of her buttocks arrested his fall. Only slightly dazed, he would have been able to climb back up, finding handholds in the heavy scarlet curtains surrounding this cascade of flesh. But up there at the top of the mountain Solange, irritated by all the prickling, sighed and, shifting the great mass of her body at an incredible speed for her weight, turned over on her right side and brought her legs together over poor Léon, who was wedged in, like a fly squashed between the pages of a book, his nose stuck in a place it would be indelicate to name.

When Solange found him in the morning, suffocated between her thighs and half dead, she was indignant and concerned in equal measure. He was all sticky and she picked him up and revived him by dunking him in a glass of ice-cold water, then in one of boiling hot water and gave him mouth-to mouth resuscitation with a straw. She blew so hard he almost burst. She could have asked Dubbelviz to help, but to have to explain that Léon slept with her would have offended the eminent professor, especially since the previous day he had asked her to marry him and she, weary of resisting, had said yes. As soon as the corpuscle had recovered, she gave vent to her fury. He had betrayed her confidence, indulged in disgusting acts. She had a good mind to spank his bottom to teach him some manners. From now on the lascivious Lilliputian was going to sleep by himself. No more night-time cuddles! His state of grace was over.

11

Daddy Flips his Lid

Once her anger had subsided, Solange bought Léon a replacement for the Jaguar, a Cessna Biplane with a real little engine that could be flown manually or by remote control. No longer being able to drive, her little husband would fly. It was a time of revived enthusiasm in the family. As if by a miracle, all the grievances and tribulations of the past months were forgotten and parents and children came together for what became a family project. Baptiste had envied his father the splendid car, but not this plane. The machine came in separate pieces and Léon helped Solange and the children to assemble it, supervising the operation with a constant stream of advice and encouragement. He couldn't sleep, he was so excited, and made up a bed at the assembly plant itself, on a bit of the kitchen table, surrounded by screwdrivers, pots of varnish, scissors. Working amid odours of turpentine and glue, he screwed, bolted and hammered relentlessly. He painted the fuselage himself, writing on it the name of his plane: Lightning.

This time Baptiste and Betty seemed fascinated – this little mannikin who called himself their father could still surprise them. Even Boris and Bérénice, the eighteen-month-old twins, attempted to express their interest in their childish babble. They could see movement, excitement and wanted to be part of it. Léon, the Waste of Space, the Weed, the Offcut, was once more given some respect by his nearest and dearest! The buzz of the undertaking, the sense of adventure, erased from his mind the memory of his recent fall from grace and banishment from the conjugal body. He was convinced that, if he kept his nose clean, Solange would eventually take him back into her pyjama pocket. To console himself, he had stolen one of her little perfumed handkerchiefs out of which he had made himself a bedspread and two pillowcases.

The aeroplane had twin carburettors which were filled with ten drops of lighter fuel. For Léon it was a fresh start, full of thrills that made him forget his recent setbacks. He found the mechanics of flight and the wind, the fact that air was a substance just as much as earth or water, more interesting than driving a car, that was too limiting. Baptiste had persuaded his mother to set up a railway network (HO gauge) that could carry his father on the dining-room table. Léon, standing up on the roof of a carriage or in a goods wagon, went from one diner to the other bearing the salt or a piece of bread in his tiny arms. A dethroned king retrained as a clown, he played the fool, tried to amuse his kids. Baptiste, who was in charge of the transformer, would increase or decrease the power at will; sometimes, as a challenge to his little father, he would push the lever right down. The train would zoom round the track at great speed until a gap between two sets of rails or two carriages that hadn't been properly linked would make it derail. Léon had to jump off while it was still moving, just before the crash. If he managed to land on his feet, the kids would applaud. If, however, he landed in the butter dish or went head over heels into the sugar bowl, sending up little clouds of powder, he was booed. Then Solange would grab him by the seat of his pants and dip him into a glass of water to clean him up. Léon was happy to resort to this buffoonery if it helped him renew his ties with his children and regain the affection of his wife.

Going from the sublime to the ridiculous, he would dress up as a Roman emperor, a court jester, a bullfighter, a tango dancer, a gigolo in patent-leather shoes, a boxer. In order to attract their attention he would wriggle like a worm, puff up his chest, plaster his hair down. Swaggering and strutting, the dwarf performed headstands, handstands, cartwheels. He wanted to astonish them, hold them spellbound; jumping on the keys of the piano, for example, he would play a dance tune with his feet, showing incredible dexterity. The little brats would applaud for five minutes then go away or bring the lid down on him with a thump, leaving him alone in the dark. He never took offence, always a smile, never a sigh. He gave a concert one evening, playing *Twinkle, twinkle little star* by tapping crystal goblets with chopsticks. He ran from one glass to the next, indefatigable, determined not to miss a single nuance of the melody until Solange, charmed by his efforts, started to hum the tune and the delighted tots joined in. It was a wonderfully harmonious evening.

But every morning he had to start from scratch again. In order to captivate them, he took crazy risks. He would dive from the top of a wine bottle into a jug of water; one day Boris, not intending any harm, happened to move the jug an inch or so to the side and Léon nearly fractured his skull. He escaped with severe bruising and had to go round with his head in bandages for several weeks. The important thing was that they would say, 'That Léon's some guy!' Juggling, walking a tightrope between two jars of water, performing death-defying leaps, jumping through a blazing hoop, he was always putting on a new turn under the amused gaze of Solange, who kept an eye on her brood. He let his beard and moustache grow in order to appear more virile, though all it did was to make him look like a hairy grain of rice. Nothing gave him greater pleasure than to hear his children laugh and clap their hands at his antics, to see their shining eyes. In those moments he was no longer the Bug, the Next-To-Nothing. Once Solange, having been won over, even called him My Big Fool. Three delightful words side by side that made his heart perform cartwheels.

To hear his children's laughter again, Léon did a standing jump into a pot of single cream, splashing the table in a radius of two feet all round. He stuck a soft-boiled egg over his head and ran off in all directions, leaving a trail of yellow behind him, arousing gales of laughter in his audience. Baptiste, amid loud guffaws, deliberately made his chair tip over backwards; his sister immediately copied him, hurt herself and started to whine. All hell was let loose: the twins decided to fall off their chairs as well, pulling down part of the tablecloth as they did so; four full plates broke with an indescribable crash and the soup tureen emptied itself over the carpet. While this was going on Léon, at the other end of the table, was still acting the fool, rolling in the butter and peeing on the bread. His hour had come. In the general commotion the little brats' applause encouraged him to step up his stupid tricks. Solange blew up, smacked the four children before sending them off to bed and telling Léon to go to his den and not show his face until further notice. His banishment lasted forty-eight hours. That was the trouble with Léon: he never knew when to stop.

His vainglory was to reach its peak in his exploits as a pilot. He spent weeks training, learnt the manual off by heart. In a short-sleeved shirt, a leather jacket and buckled slip-ons, he made his maiden flight at 10 am precisely on Christmas Eve, taking off from the dining-room table towards the corridor. He made several careful circuits of the room at an average height of six feet, the ceiling being eleven feet high, and came in to land a quarter of an hour later on the same runway to the cheers of the children. Solange was there with the remote control in case there was a problem. He didn't make a single error, negotiated the different atmospheric pressures perfectly, played with the winds, avoided colliding with the furniture. His aerobatics, he was sure, would make him his children's absolute hero and undermine the dubious prestige Dubbelviz was trying to acquire. Impressed by her mini-husband's mastery of the machine, Solange put the electronic control away in a cupboard.

For weeks everything went wonderfully well. As soon as the first ray of sun reached his cabin – he slept with the shutters wide open so as not to miss a moment of the light – Léon, freshly shaven (he'd got rid of the beard and moustache) and impeccably turned out in the pilot's uniform that came with the aeroplane and that he'd altered to fit himself, slid down in his toboggan. He swung the propellor by hand, in the traditional way, jumped into the aircraft that was parked on the floor in a hangar he'd put together out of cardboard boxes, throttled up and took off at around 7.30 after making a final check and filling the reserve tanks, one drop of lighter fuel in each. His room had become a real workshop with dozens of tools, each kept in its own compartment, little jars of lubricant, screwdrivers, rags covered in grease; it was there that he pampered his pride and joy. He took off after twenty inches precisely and pulled back the control column to climb, though not before he'd made sure that the boxroom door was still open, that it it hadn't been blown shut by a draught.

Once he had gained height, at least three feet above the floor, he entered the long winding corridor which took him to the living-cum-dining-room. Then he ascended to a height of six feet, skimming the ceiling lights, and did two tight turns. This was a highly skilled manoeuvre, especially for a self-taught pilot. The plane vibrated as if it were alive, part of his organism, an extension of his chest. Avoiding the huge chandelier over the table, he made a triumphant entrance into the dining room. The children were alerted to it by the hum of the engine and Baptiste, watching his father arrive through his binoculars, performed the function of the control tower. They immediately cleared the landing strip, a long, waxed bread-board, cleared of crumbs and with a wad of cotton wool attached by elastic at the end in case the brakes should fail. Léon would land with many a bump and bounce, turn and park his machine and jump out of the cockpit to the cheers of the crowd, which he would acknowledge with elegant bows. He then took his coffee in his own special seat, a doll's chair on the tarmac. How he felt his batteries recharge as he sat there sipping his espresso from half an empty acorn shell and nibbling a warm morsel of croissant dipped in bramble jam!

After a few weeks he started doing risky manoeuvres, taking off from shorter distances, hedgehopping over the children's beds, buzzing round the television, criss-crossing the screen with his constant nosedives, shouted at by the children, who couldn't watch their programmes. He over-revved the engine, the cockpit keeled over, he made crazy bets with himself: land on the narrow top of a chair-back, on the arms of a chair. Without realising it, he was exasperating his children by his frenetic urge to amaze them. They began to talk to him as if he were simple-minded: you noisy, you no drive plane now, you go away.

His plane left a wake of white steam behind it and one day he managed, with a series of dizzying rolls and loops, twisting and turning between the lamps and the doorframe, to write: I LOVE YOU ALL. But the older children had just gone out with Solange to clean their teeth, so that only Boris and Bérénice, who couldn't read, saw the inscription, that was immediately blown away by a puff of wind. Modest to the point of arrogance, puny to the point of monstrosity, he was like one of the little characters stuck at the bottom of strip cartoons that contort themselves and stick out their tongue to attract our attention.

Having nothing to offer his offspring apart from his silly pranks, he ended up overdoing things. For example he would burst into the kitchen on his flying machine, terrorise the nanny, pull out a lock of her hair as he swept past her – there you are, take that, you pest, you bitch – fly round the pans and the stove, checking on the cooking with his binoculars, shouting into his radio: boiled eggs ready, spaghetti cooked, minced beef rare, over to you, Ground Control! He was not without his spiteful moments: he broke into his wife's bedroom, saw a gorilla wearing pyjamas sprawled out on Solange's bed with its arms round his own children that were snuggling up to it. Professor Dubbelviz, covered in a layer of black hair on his shoulders and back and a real carpet over his buttocks, was now officially engaged to Solange; he slept in His bed, drank in His chair, took His wife in his arms. What's the use of a father if he can be replaced that quickly? Léon went into a dive, fired his machine guns: GET OFF MY PILLOW, YOU FAT LUMP, TUB OF LARD, CHOLESTEROL JUNKIE. Dubbelviz just had time to roll off onto the floor and escape to the bathroom and lock himself in the lavatory.

'Help, Solange! He's trying to kill me!'

'Oh, come on, darling, he's only four inches high, not much more than twice the size of your penis.'

'He's armed, he's firing real grains of rice, he could hit me in the eye, blind me. It's the Napoleon syndrome, the midgets' desire for revenge, it's well-known.'

To tell the truth, Dubbelviz was in a difficult position: marrying a woman whose ex-husband, reduced to the size of a lizard, is still living in the marital home requires an unusual degree of open-mindedness. Tired of his intrusions, Solange banned Léon from her bedroom.

He imagined himself one of the pioneers of flight crossing the Andes or the oceans in a flimsy crate, the heir to Mermoz or Lindbergh, he could already see himself leading a squadron. He pampered his machine, spoke to it, urged it on and constantly added technical improvements. Now he was dreaming of a jet, a Rafale or an F–16, and regretted having studied medicine instead of training to be a fighter pilot.

12

The Unforgivable Sin

One fine, mild day in February Léon, whose aerobatic achievements had gone to his head, decided to go for broke. Taking advantage of the sunshine and the wide-open windows in the sitting room – they were airing the apartment – he flew straight out into the wide world of the city. Crossing the balustrade of the balcony, he found himself 100 feet above the cars and buses down below. It was more than a year now that he'd been confined to the apartment and it gave him a shock. Blinded by a flash of light, he closed his eyes and leant his head back on the leather seat.

He was gripped by a wild dream of freedom. He had so badly missed the sounds and colours of Paris; he had forgotten how beautiful it was. He weaved his way through the electric cables, straightened up to lift himself over the tops of the trees, bare chestnuts with precocious buds already appearing, passed a low-flying flock of swallows, frightened a seagull, saw the schoolchildren playing in the park below and, after two or three loop-the-loops worthy of an ace pilot, headed back for the sitting room.

But he was careless and didn't check his route properly so that instead of going home he flew into the apartment of the neighbours, a cantankerous couple, pensioners by the nickname of Arsepain with whom Solange had very strained relations. They were enjoying lunch in the sunshine by their double window, that was also open, and were terrified at the appearance of the crazy pilot. Believing they were being attacked by hornets they started to bombard him with chicken bones, brussels sprouts and sauté potatoes. Blinded by these missiles, the intensive anti-aircraft fire, his crate covered in gravy – oh, that horrible mess on the elegant oval of the fuselage! – Léon went into a dive, straightened up just in time, managed to avoid crashing into the shelves of leather-bound books, half of which concealed bottles of alcohol, banked and headed out into the open air, away from these barbarians who did not appreciate his aerobatics.

He recognised his own balcony from the white roses that had come into flower again in the middle of winter, the tubs of box, the huge, scratched green watering can, the shelters for birds which the children had made out of clay, but a gust of wind blew him off course and sent him plunging down. Enormous clouds were coming from the north east, harbingers of wintry weather, of rain or snow. There was nothing like this turbulence in the apartment, he had great trouble dealing with it, not having made it part of his apprenticeship. The force of the squally wind, the suddenly darkened sky, made him all too aware of his diminutive size. Taking advantage of a brief lull, he managed to hold the plane but, being short of fuel, had to do an emergency landing on the rutted concrete of the balcony, between two grow-bags.

The wheels broke under the impact, the plane cartwheeled, ending up on its side, and the port wing broke in two. To add to his mortification Josiane, noticing how cold it was getting, had closed the window. Léon could have sworn she'd seen him and had deliberately looked away, taking advantage of this piece of luck to leave him to die outside. Bruised, shaking with fear, wearing only a pair of light flannel trousers and a polo shirt, Léon was left shivering outside for hours. After all, it was winter. A storm was brewing, the temperature was getting lower by the minute, as can often happen in Paris. He spent the afternoon hammering on the windows with all the strength his little fists were capable of. When she finally discovered him, as she was shaking out the tablecloth, Solange scolded him and confined him to his room for twenty-four hours. All the children, with that affectation of solemnity with which they imitate adults, told him off, including Boris and Bérénice, babbling in their infants' Esperanto. They were beginning to find this creature a real pain and told him to shut up as soon as he tried to plead his case. What was even more worrying: he had disappeared for over six hours and no one missed him. It no longer mattered whether he was there or not.

The spell was broken and Léon had been reduced to the status of a pedestrian, that is, an ordinary mortal. He had to go back to making his way round the gigantic apartment on foot, risking being trodden on by one of the Biggies at every corner. He could, like tourist guides, have carried a flag alerting them to his presence. It took hours to go anywhere. He felt humiliated when Baptiste, suddenly struck down with an excruciatingly painful ear infection, was taken by his mother to the A & E at Necker Hospital without him, who was, after all, a specialist, having not been consulted at all. So he stayed quietly in his room, going vroom, vroom, bzz, bzz, dreaming of flying across continents, dive-bombing, imagining himself in command of a B–52 flattening the apartment with bombs, setting the carpets on fire with phosphorus and napalm, dispatching the nanny with a single rocket to her hair, that would then catch fire, forcing Dubbelviz to surrender, sending him scuttling down the stairs in his socks and underpants.

Solange did at least give him one last chance: she had the

aeroplane repaired in a shop specialising in models. But she issued a new decree: henceforth the pilot would be limited to flights from his boxroom to the sitting room and back. The other rooms were closed to air traffic. Any infraction of this regulation would result in the confiscation of the machine that would then be thrown out or even destroyed depending on the decision of the committee responsible (of which she was chairwoman and sole member). Léon swore, Léon promised – and hardly had he been restored to his position of flying fool than he forgot everything. Up there, alone in the stratosphere, the stupid orders of an earth-bound creature meant nothing. Beneath him he could see the tops of his children's heads, the boys' unruly tufts, the girls' neatly tied plaits, he could have taken some magnificent pictures of them: the earth seen from the sky; he took himself for an eagle contemplating the dull herd of humans. Providence had chosen him from among all men and had only brought him down in order to raise him up even higher. He would go his own sweet way and the inhabitants of the apartment had better watch out.

One evening the disaster happened. Whether he was tired or had had a dram too many – oh yes, Léon had started to drink, stealing Dubbelviz's whisky – he took off from his private airstrip at dinner time without having checked his reserve tanks under the wings, each of which held one drop of petrol. The biplane quickly ran out of fuel. As he was proudly coming through the door to the dining room, where the whole tribe was eating under the benevolent dictatorship of Dubbelviz, who was commentating on a football match, the engine started to splutter with a series of horrible hiccoughs, as if it were about to give up the ghost. Panicking, Léon sent out distress signals over the radio but unfortunately the air-traffic controllers were having their dinner break and didn't reply. He tried to execute a turn above the chandelier, an impressive Venetian wedding-cake structure, all pendants and sparkling crystal, that Dubbelviz had given Solange as an engagement present. Losing momentum, the engine not responding any more, the plane didn't make the turn, went into a nose-dive and crashed right into the majestic piece of architecture, which exploded in a thousand shards and started to swing dangerously over the table.

It wasn't just a crash, it was an absolute disaster. Glass and gemstones rained down on the plates, the glasses, the serving dishes. Solange, the children and Dubbelviz all cried out in unison: THE CHANDELIER! The professor's instinctive reaction was to push the children and his dear fiancée down under the table where they could shelter from the projectiles. Not content with having demolished his aeroplane, Léon had suffered serious injuries: cuts above the eyes, broken ribs, lacerated cheeks. Pushing himself up on a brass rod, he managed to get out of the cockpit and prepared to parachute down, but due to his dizziness, he lost his footing. He tried to grab a piece of the fuselage, missed it and plummeted into the soup steaming below, alphabet noodles spiced up with a touch of paprika, Dubbelviz's favourite.

There was a big splash. He swallowed a mouthful of soup, hit the bottom and resurfaced among a flotsam of letters, his mouth full of strands of leeks and bits of carrot. He was choking, he called for help. The hailstorm of crystal droplets had stopped, the chandelier was swaying to and fro like an out-of-control airship. The thwarted diners emerged from underneath the table, assessing the extent of the cataclysm. Dubbelviz took charge of operations. With repeated instructions to the others to be careful, he went to fetch some stepladders. As one, the four children peered over the rim of the soup tureen and in their shifty, exasperated looks Léon could read the same thought: Why don't we just go ahead and drown him? It was a moment of horror in which four adorable little faces pronounced a sentence of death. They hovered round him like the grim faces of the Four Horsemen of the Apocalypse. Josiane joined them and placed her large, red forefinger on his head. But Solange, forgiving, arrived in time to save him, fished him out with a coffee spoon and dropped him in a fingerbowl, where he ended up like a shipwrecked sailor, more dead than alive.

She didn't say a word. With a set expression on her face, her lips blue they were pressed together so tight, she dumped him in his cupboard like a piece of rubbish and locked the door.

Part 3

Distress and Redemption

13

The Hooligan Banished

In few moments Léon had lost everything, first and foremost Solange's indulgence. Sickened by the destruction of the chandelier, she resolved to have done with this homunculus who bore no relation to her former husband in his many forms, and no longer even had that fantastic protuberance that used to delight her so. In his extravagant behaviour she saw the operation of a law according to which the mess created by a person is in inverse proportion to his size. She now regarded him as a nuisance, a sort of insect that was all the more worrying because it was hardly visible. Some demon had played a nasty trick on them, bringing misfortune to the family, and Solange, like Josiane, was wondering if Léon were not the work of the devil, sent to try them. Dubbelviz was urging her to put an end to the situation. Léon was officially dead, the important thing now was to quietly get him away from the children, for example drop him down the lavatory and pull the chain. Solange's religious belief was too strong for her to resort to such extreme action.

She abandoned this bizarre fellow, like a toy that had had its uses but was no longer amusing, and sentenced him to life imprisonment. She no longer wanted to have anything to do with this apology for a husband. The children were unanimous in their agreement, giving free rein to their resentment of the Runt. The idea that he could have played a part in fathering them seemed highly improbable. How could they see the least connection between themselves and Léon, tell themselves that there had been a time when this pipsqueak had made their mother pregnant, that they were the offspring of their tumultuous embraces, when Solange was huge enough to accommodate all four of them inside her, even now when Baptiste was eight and the twins two. There was only one head of the family and that was their mother, whose character and strength commanded fear and respect and the acceptance of her new lover, Professor Dubbelviz. Each one of them was given strict orders never to let the word 'Daddy' – a coarse word, an obscene word – cross their lips in public: if they no longer mentioned him, he would eventually disappear for good. He thereafter vanished from their conversations but at night every one of them dreamt of him.

Inconsolable at the loss of her chandelier and suffering from stress, Solange bought, on Dubbelviz's advice, a machine to tire the children out. You know the kind of thing, every school has one for hyperactive children. It's like a spin dryer, only much bigger, since you can put three bodies into it at a time. You place the subjects in a rotating cylinder, attaching them to the drum by straps so that they won't fall on each other, and programme it according to the required degree of exhaustion: dog-tired, dead-tired, more dead than alive. Subjected to rapid rotation, the guinea pigs lose consciousness and only wake up at the end of the session to go to bed. The four children were given a whirl in it on Saturdays and Sundays, despite their horror of the machine, Baptiste, the biggest, on his own, the three younger ones together. Léon shivered as he listened to their cries.

He really would have liked to be able to prevent Solange from going to such an extreme that was, moreover, legal since the apparatus, called the Exhauster, could tire boisterous children out better than any TV programme or video game. Solange even took a turn in it herself when she suffered from insomnia or anxiety and would crawl out to drag herself off to bed.

At the beginning of his incarceration Léon still received meagre rations delivered by a sarcastic Josiane, who would open the door and put down a bowl containing three grains of rice, a segment of orange, a crust of bread. Gone were the days of roast ortolan and vintage wines, delicacies and tangy cheeses. After two weeks, this room service stopped abruptly. Léon realised he hadn't been put into solitary confinement as a brief punishment but had been locked away for good. Fortunately, during his days of glory he had built up a little hoard of basic provisions. Starting as his wife's husband, he had become her son, then his children's plaything, before ending up as vermin which the whole family wanted to eradicate. He was destined to wander eternally, on the edges of the world of men, trapped in a fissure of time. The door remained locked, he was gone and forgotten. He called out, screamed, 'I'm hungry, I'm starving, I'm famished!' His voice was absorbed by the plaster on the walls. Even the cat, he thought, had stopped pursuing him, scratching at the door and miaowing, as if it no longer regarded him as a choice morsel.

Delicious smells of gratin dauphinois, veal Marengo, courgette soup, tagine reached him; his stomach howled, his mouth salivated, his teeth chattered. Ensconced in his cell, he developed incredibly acute hearing: the rumble of the métro starting at five in the morning, the soft moan of a door swinging in the wind, the creak of floorboards, the distant mechanism of the lift all allowed him to share in the life of the building. The drip-drip of a leaky tap set off explosions that gave him a headache, the gurgle of the plumbing signalled the hour of ablutions, he knew when someone gargled in the flat below. He could follow the rhythms of family life: the children going off to school, Josiane's heavy tread as she cleaned the apartment, Solange and Dubbelviz coming back from work, Baptiste and Betty squabbling, the twins babbling in their pidgin French. Solange's delicate perfume hung around the apartment. At night he even caught the sound of heavy breathing from the conjugal bedroom that churned him up inside. For most of the day silence reigned. He and Furbelow shared the same territory, unaware of each other, though he did have the feeling that sometimes the cat came and sat outside the door, listening, trying to renew a link.

He had to admit: they got on very well without him. He'd never been indispensable. Life went on. He became very depressed, wandering round among the suitcases that had come apart at the hinges, broken toys, old, stained clothes kept for the poor of the district. The immense, chaotic landscape frightened him. Lumps of plaster the size of rocks threatened to fall off the ceiling, the walls, damp from leaks, had huge cracks. He was naked and alone in this icy desert. He was like a piece of rubbish himself, a withered little package of skin and bones reduced to his animal instincts. He felt he was at one with the tramps and beggars who went from place to place, forced to move on by respectable people. Except that he was a prisoner in his own home, imprisoned in his own body. He spent three whole days in delirium, lying in the fetid dust. He felt he was dying, abandoned by everyone, reduced to the status of an invertebrate. He was hungry and hunger deprived him of his dignity, turned him into a wild beast.

Fortunately it was summer, abounding in insect life: flies, midges, butterflies, bees, cockroaches, death-watch beetles, grubs. They seemed to emerge from everywhere, by spontaneous generation, from the floor as much as from the plaster on the walls. With a spear made from a hairpin he killed columns of ants that were attacking a crumb of bread. The large green flies he stabbed in the back as they clung to the window, buzzing like bombers, crucified and devoured them, still quivering, their wings fluttering against his palate. He attacked the moths with their stringy consistency, their powdery thoraxes, biting into them with repugnance, his mind having retained the tastes and distastes of a human being. A cloud of midges, hanging in the evening air, lasted him for two days. He would have liked a few more cockroaches, just to vary his menu. Once he had a fierce duel with a little wasp that had found its way there; he made a trap by rubbing his skin with a sugar crystal and impaled it from below, avoiding its deadly sting. To him the insect's death seemed long and painful. Given his own size, he found the suffering of a tiny creature no less unbearable than that of a human being. One morning a scarab, a little jewel of gold and crimson fell into the room. He spared it as a tribute to its beauty.

He was completely taken up with the question of survival: he had erased all humanity from inside himself, he soldiered on in rags and filth. Always on the alert, skin black with dirt, hands and feet covered in calluses, scalp covered in scabs, he was like a creature from the Stone Age with his loincloth and spear. Furious at his weakness, he subjected himself to a relentless programme of physical exercise. He taught himself to climb and used pieces of sewing thread and string to make little ropes so that he could climb easily across the walls. At the end of a month of intensive training, he had turned himself into a lively, nervous little monkey hiding in the curtain rods, the cornices, the lining of a torn leather suitcase, scampering from one peak to the next, a kind of gladiator armed with net and spear, always ready to eliminate anything that got in his way. If he had to die, he would sell his life dearly. He was waging all-out war against the world, against himself.

14

Attempted Pygmicide

Léon woke one morning with a sense of foreboding. They were conspiring against him, he could tell. Solange had become obsessed with the idea of getting rid of the microbe. She was Catholic but she was also superstitious: she dreaded the souls of the dead that came back to haunt certain houses, calling for revenge. She was terrified by the fact that Léon, because of his size, could squeeze through anywhere. Dubbelviz and Josiane helped her to overcome her scruples. It wouldn't be murder since everyone thought he was already dead. She spent a long time in prayer, asking God's forgiveness in advance. Then she organised a commando raid.

At midnight precisely, taking advantage of the fact that all four children were sleeping at their grandparents', Solange and Josiane, helmeted and their faces painted white, besieged the cubbyhole. Dubbelviz was covering them from the corridor, armed with a spade. Their faces contorted with hatred and fear, the two furies flung open the door, trained a powerful torch on every inch of the place and exploded into action, smashing everything there was to smash with hammers and spraying the boxroom with a powerful insecticide. After seven minutes the operation was called off and the attack team withdrew since the air had become unbreathable.

'No doubt about it,' Dubbelviz said, 'the rubbish has had it.'

Just to make sure, they were going to mount another attack

the next day.

Fortunately Léon was expecting them. During the last few days he had heard too much whispering outside his door not to be worried. He had prepared an escape plan and was on the look out for the enemy. He crouched underneath a large flake of plaster which, providentially, had fallen off the ceiling just by the entrance to the room, beside a socket that had been pulled out of the wall. He had rehearsed the moment a hundred times: he would only have a few seconds to escape. Hardly had Solange and Josiane entered the boxroom than he slipped out, crawling, into the corridor and hid, without being seen by Dubbelviz, underneath the big draught excluder. At the awful sounds of the furious attack he stuck his fingers in his ears and was half asphyxiated by the spray. He held on despite the racket, the stamping of the two women, Dubbelviz's cries of encouragement.

It must have been half past twelve when the two women, exhausted by their fury and amazed at their own savagery, went to bed. Solange was crying, Dubbelviz consoling her, repeating, 'The nightmare's over.' Léon, staggered out from underneath the draught excluder and ventured into the vastness of the canyon-like corridor. He felt dizzy and had to lean against the wall. He was hungry and automatically headed for the kitchen. First of all he had to get something inside himself, he'd think about what to do after that: he'd just managed to escape being killed, but it was only a temporary reprieve. Getting to the other end of the apartment took a good hour. Any little creak threw him into a panic, he expected to see Josiane or Solange burst out of one of the rooms to flatten him with a fly swatter. He fell to his knees several times, tempted to let himself be killed, then got up again. He was so weak that hardly had he got to the vast kitchen than he fell upon the cat's food that was on a plate beside the rubbish bin. He was incapable of even trying to climb up onto the stainless-steel table that towered up above him, cold and metallic and on which, as he remembered, there was always a little bowl of fresh fruit, summer and winter. Furbelow's dinner consisted of a sticky mass of meat lumps giving off a fetid odour that turned his stomach. He regretted not having paid more attention to the cat's food in the days when he was still capable of doing so – he would have prohibited such stinking factory-made mush. He was stuffing himself with this nauseating fodder, eating with his hands, when a huge shadow cast by the orange light of the street lamps outside moved across the floor in front of him until it covered him entirely. He started, looked up from his swill, that he was crouching over on all fours, and wiped his mouth on his sleeve. Two luminous beacons went on: a large sphinx, sitting on its haunches, had fixed its gaze on him.

Furbelow! Léon yelped in fright. He could smell the pungent odour of the cat's slightly bouffant coat. A deadly silence ensued. The beast had found him, had crept up behind him without a sound. It looked at him, licking its chops now and then, languidly putting out its tongue on the right and on the left, revealing long, white teeth. Léon could already feel its claws raking his skin and the bite that would break his neck. He saw himself as a prey cornered by a killer. Dripping with fat, he got off the plate and looked the cat up and down, arms crossed, ready to die standing up. He'd forgotten to bring his spear. He waved his arms round and round to frighten Furbelow. It just gave a sinister growl and stretched its neck; its two eyes, like glowing embers, fixed on him. He could see himself, a pathetic warrior, imprinted on the retina of the animal, whose pupils had contracted to a slit. It spat, emitted a quavering miaow, raised one paw, unsheathed its claws.The end had come.

But the paw dropped back onto the floor. A hoarse rumbling sound came from the cat's throat. It was some time before Léon realised that Furbelow was purring, that its intentions were not belligerent at all. It even seemed to sympathise with its former master, who had been reduced to stealing its food.

Then something unexpected happened. Taking a run-up, it jumped onto the kitchen table, grasped a fruit from the bowl, pushed it to the edge with its paw and made it fall down. It was a very ripe peach, just starting to go bad on one side, that hit the floor with the thud of a soft bomb in a splatter of juice and flesh. Léon understood at once, threw himself on the fruit and tunnelled into it, like a miner driving a hole in the rock, feet, hands and chest immersed in the flesh running with syrupy juice. He thanked the cat, that was watching him eat, and, sticky with peach as he was, asked it, 'So what now, where do I sleep?' Furbelow miaowed softly and, in a kind of tacit agreement, led him to the bathroom where its basket was. Léon climbed up into it and hid under an old woollen rag covered in cat-hair, satiated, drowsy and sure that providence was on his side and would protect him from all future danger. Before falling asleep he realised, to his shame, that the cat had never attacked him, had never taken advantage of its physical superiority. He resolved to ask it to forgive him for his suspicions in the morning.

15

A Show of Solidarity

Léon shared Furbelow's basket for a week. During the day he went to hide under the bathtub, behind the inspection hatch, the tiled panel of which had cracked, leaving a narrow gap he could squeeze through. There was a whole tangle of pipes there and the noise was deafening. Every evening, as soon as the family were asleep, the cat would knock down an apple, a sugar lump, a cherry tomato, even nuts that broke on the tiled floor so that Léon could extract the kernel from the bits of shell. He stored these victuals underneath the bath, eating what was perishable first, fighting off the insects and parasites that were proliferating in the heat of June. Furbelow also tried to steal the odd crust of bread or piece of meat, fishing scraps of pot-au-feu, osso buco, bouillabaisse out of the pan left on the cooker that Léon then ate warm or cold. The cook soon noticed these little thefts from the trail of gravy they left behind and from then on put the food somewhere safe, not without having first given Furbelow a good hiding.

The cat didn't always have a clear idea of humans' dietary range, but its devotion saved Léon's life, letting him lap up the milk in its bowl once it had had a drink itself. Mini-man was deeply moved by its generosity, all the more so since he drew lessons in animal wisdom from it. With its calmness, it seemed to be saying, 'Don't moan, hold out, learn patience.' Now Furbelow and Léon were inseparable: the Half Pint would scratch the cat's stomach with a doll's comb and, stretched out between its ears, massage its head, sending shivers rippling all along the animal's spine while it purred like a speedboat engine. The steward of the pocket kingdom was no longer alone, he was assisted by a mustachioed giant. As soon as the house was asleep, Furbelow would lie down to let Léon climb up and sit astride its neck. Gripping its silky coat, he would be carried round the apartment, like a rajah on his elephant. The cat would trot along at a lively pace and Léon loved these midnight excursions.

He had to find a safe place to stay. Sooner or later Josiane or the children would flush him out of the cat's basket and that would be the end of him. Léon gave it intense thought.

What is the best hiding-place in a modern apartment, better than a cellar, a boxroom, a loft?

Where does people's indifference protect one better than in a bunker?

What is visible for all and yet invisible to everyone?

What is an absolutely useless place no one's interested in, that's just part of the furniture?

It didn't take long to find the answer: the bookshelves, naturally.

And on bookshelves who are the authors that are never opened, even if people claim to have read them? Bestsellers? Guidebooks? Cookery books? Encyclopaedias? No, the classics, of course. And which of the classics are the ones people always talk about without ever opening them? Léon was spoilt for choice. As it happened, Solange had put all her school and university books on the bottom shelves in her study. They were the beautiful bound volumes of a middle-class child who was given the best editions as presents. Proust, Tolstoy, Zola, Hugo, Joyce and Dickens shared a shelf with

Balzac, Flaubert, Dostoyevsky, the Bible, Sartre, Hegel and Kant in a long, tall row of quarto volumes.

He hesitated for a long time between all these giants before finally deciding on the last: it was a simple matter of thickness and paper quality. The frayed binding, the faded print – not from having been consulted too often but from having been abandoned, worn away by cold, heat and humidity – would make his work easier. So one night, armed with a piece of a razor blade, he made a small home for himself in the hundreds of pages of the *Critique of Judgment* by cutting out several chapters between 'The Analytic of the Beautiful' and 'The Analytic of the Sublime' and turned it into a cosy nest. It was an exhausting task which demanded all his skills as an architect and a rodent, as ingenious as that of a prisoner digging a tunnel beneath his cell to escape. During his excavations he came across sentences of an unheard-of profundity that made him dizzy and others he didn't agree with at all. Solange had underlined some with a yellow felt-tip, scribbling notes in the margin. She must have been a model pupil.

These tombstones of paper and glue made an ideal hideout for a being of his size. He disposed of the debris carefully, dispersing it all over the apartment so that no one would suspect what was going on. He was slightly ashamed of hacking into the living flesh of the great classics but, small though he was, he needed the space. With time he extended his residence into the neighbouring volumes, cutting doors in the covers, hollowing out a corridor between each of them so that soon he was living in a paper palace with numerous rooms, going from *Les Misérables* to *War and Peace* via *The Brothers Karamazov*, *Phenomenology of Spirit*, *Finding Time Again*. Very comfortable, *War and Peace*, thick walls, solid vellum, a delightful, slightly faded fragrance. And Dickens, what a

117

good sleep he got chez Dickens, so quiet. *Oliver Twist, The Pickwick Papers,* ideal for insomniacs, what good vibrations. The same with Joyce: hardly had he stretched out in *Ulysses* than he was snoring away and nothing could disturb his sleep. He would sometimes catch a long sentence on a wall, learn it off by heart and savour it like a stroke of genius. Living inside these masterpieces stimulated his mind, broadened his horizons, put him at the heart of world literature, even though he was worried that after several months in that abode his blood might turn to ink. He went for walks in the books he liked, swearing he would read them from end to end once there were miniature editions of them. He would, of course, have been more comfortable in Robert's *Dictionnaire de la langue française,* the *Larousse* or the *Encyclopaedia Britannica,* which had a whole shelf to itself. But that was a risk it wasn't worth taking since dictionaries can get consulted from time to time.

Léon slept during the day and only got up when Solange and Dubbelviz came back from work. A stowaway who saw everything without being seen, Léon participated in the life of the family, followed the children, recognising them from their voices. Solange went through their homework with them. Sometimes she was stumped by a problem to which Léon knew the answer and he had to stop himself jumping out into the room and whispering it to her. From what he could tell – the conversations he heard were muffled – Baptiste was going to have to repeat a year and Betty was already overweight. He was very sad about that.

He would go out at night to find sustenance. Fortunately Solange was always snacking in her study, shelling almonds and hazelnuts, chomping away at a cracker or a biscuit while she checked her emails, dropping crumbs on the floor on which he later feasted. The effect was rather like that of those birds that peck at the remains of food stuck between crocodiles' or hippopotamuses' teeth. His wife was still feeding him while she thought he was dead, a foster mother despite herself. Unless... unless she knew and was deliberately dropping the morsels as a subtle expression of love? That was what he liked to think.

Safe though he was, Léon was far from happy. He was surviving as an outcast whose slightest mistake could be fatal. One evening he asked the cat for a special favour (they communicated by signs and managed to make themselves understood): he wanted to have a closer look at his two older children, Baptiste and Betty, the only ones with whom he had shared the experience of fatherhood. During the day, crouching between two books, all he could see was their legs, their fat calves, already, in Baptiste's case, covered in blond downy hair and scars. With a mighty leap Furbelow deposited him on the children's bedside table, in the middle of construction sets, dolls with dead, permanently astonished eyes, a squad of lead soldiers with bayonets fixed and standards raised.

Baptiste had accumulated a splendid collection of infantry and cavalry he'd bought out of his pocket money in a little shop in the Palais-Royal. The two children slept in parallel beds, but that evening Betty, after suffering a nightmare, had taken refuge in her elder brother's bed. They lived under the tyrannical rule of clocks: everywhere there was the grating tick-tock of huge Mickey-Mouse alarm clocks, pendulum clocks, smiling cuckoo clocks, stopwatches, luminous watches all out of tune with each other. None showed the same time or followed the same rhythm. Having entered the snake-pit, Léon settled down between a hussar and a grenadier in a bearskin and, deeply moved, watched his children who were sleeping peacefully. The brats had settled down in a charming heap, arms and legs intertwined. Sleeping, they had angelic faces with relaxed features, round, pink cheeks and half-open mouths with the tips of their tongues sticking out. God, how beautiful, pure and innocent they were! He would have liked to grasp the little darlings with both hands, ruffle their hair, cover them in kisses. Their bodies, lying in graceful postures, gave off a sweet warmth. Faced with this, he couldn't keep back his silent tears. They were there, close to him but farther away than if they were separated by an ocean, beings of a different line, a different humanity. It would always be like that.

A papal guard, holding his halberd, whispered, 'It's tough, isn't it, when you're the father, they're so cute. Then one day, off they go and leave us for good.'

Léon nodded in reply, showing no surprise that a lump of painted metal could speak to him in his own language. After all, he himself had become a kind of chatterbox toy, they understood each other as people of the same species. He sobbed even more, moving the tin army to tears as well, the Spahis, Uhlans, those veterans who in their time had seen much worse. But they were decent guys, despite everything, with their hearts in the right place, guys who had looked death in the face. Towards four in the morning Léon started talking out loud to his sleeping son; the troops, sitting cross-legged, had formed a protective circle round him, revolvers and cartridges on the ground. He didn't seem to feel embarrassed by the presence of all these strangers.

'I know I haven't been able to devote much time to you, Baptiste, apart from the first years, but it's not my fault, you know, I lost my body very quickly and, believe me, I would have preferred to have kept it so that I could bring all of you up, including the last two, who are completely lost to me. You are the only one with whom I had a brief experience of being a father, and I can assure that it still fills me with wonder. I embarrassed you. You used to say, "My father's a little squirt," and you forbade me from coming and meeting you at the end of school or from going for walks with you in the street. I can understand that, I would have reacted in the same way. But you're still the best thing I did in this world…'

He spoke for a long time, out of breath, told Baptiste about his broken dreams, his frustrated aspirations, advised him to support his mother, to love the man who had succeeded him. He enjoined him not to treat his brother and sisters roughly, to work hard at school and finally expressed the hope that he wouldn't leave him with too bad a memory of his father. While he was talking, in such a low voice even the soldiers were forced to strain their ears to understand him, the two children muttered in their sleep, tossed and turned, sobbed and cried out now and then. As soon as daylight started to shine through the curtains, waking the exotic birds on the wallpaper, Léon saluted the gallant soldiers, his companions in misfortune, closed his eyes and slid down onto Furbelow's spine; the cat carried him back to his abode.

16

Going to the Aid of the Weak

Summer had just begun. As happened every year, a torrid heat wave had settled over the capital, slowing down the people, their activities. As soon as school had finished, the family went off on holiday to the seaside in Brittany. Léon was alone with Furbelow, whom the concierge came to feed every evening at around six. He felt abandoned; the departure of the others left him depressed. He could no longer bear this subterranean life. He would give himself up when the children came back and if they exterminated him, so be it. At least he would die at their hands if he couldn't live on their caresses.

It was at that time that an unusual event occurred. One afternoon, the fourth of July, a raging storm, preceded by violent gusts of wind, burst over Paris, plunging it into darkness after a few minutes. The rain pelted down on the windows, streamed over the walls in torrents, darkened the tiles. Léon, standing on the kitchen radiator that he had just climbed up, took advantage of the fact that the window had been left slightly open to take a shower in the spray from the downpour, vaguely hoping that it might make him get bigger, as it made the plants grow. Suddenly, in the middle of the general din, he thought he heard a cry from outside, different from the loud splatter of the raindrops. A sort of chirping, a shrill sound that also alerted the cat that, crouching under the table out of fear of the lightning, had pricked up its ears and sat up. He wiped off the condensation so that he could see more clearly and had the impression that there was a fierce scuffle going on not far away.

Now he could see better: it was a fight between birds. A fat crow with a beak as sharp as an ice-pick was fighting over a scrap of food with a tit that had been caught in the anti-pigeon net over the courtyard of the block of flats. A titanic struggle over a morsel of bread ensued, feathers flying in the deluge. The crow wasn't simply trying to steal the tit's food, it was pecking at it in order to kill it. The smaller bird was weakening, wailing pathetically. Léon did not hesitate for one moment, he was incensed by any situation in which a small creature was oppressed by a bigger one. He had nothing to lose, he just followed his heart. Remembering how Furbelow had helped him when he was starving, he slipped through the narrow opening of the window, encouraged by the cat that was making little throaty growls, quivering with desire, perhaps hoping it would soon be devouring the creatures that were squabbling so close to it; crow or tit, it would have been happy with either.

Léon had equipped himself with shoes with a good grip, an ice-axe he'd made out of a drawing pin and a coil of cord he'd taken from his climbing kit. Belayed to a little metal projection, he let himself down to the net that was fixed at the bottom of that storey, like a spider setting off to collect its prey in the middle of its web, and crawled across it, lozenge by lozenge, glad that the net had such a fine mesh, to reach the bird in distress. Each drop of rain had the density of a stone and threatened to knock him off – when you're so small how can you resist a heavy shower like that? The wind shook the net. He almost lost his grip more than once, just managing to hold on at the last minute. Ignoring the lashing rain, he concentrated on the metal rungs of the ladders for the chimney sweeps, the aerials twisted by the wind, the round chimney pots. He inched his way forward; the water made the handholds slippery, the nylon cut into his palms. If he looked down, the dizzy height made his stomach turn: hundreds of miles below him the earth – in the form of a tenement courtyard, four yellow and green rubbish bins and puny plants which the concierge was trying to grow in wooden tubs – was sucking him down. The drop was calling to him like the black maw of hell, begging him to jump: it would be the end of all his worries, his derisory existence. He concentrated on his task, afraid of getting there too late.

It took a grimly determined effort but he reached the birds. The tit was injured, one of its wings broken, leaving a trickle of blood on its downy feathers. The poor little thing was emitting pitiful cheeps. In panic, its blue-green eye was spinning round and round in the socket like a billiard ball gone mad. The crow was preparing to give it the coup de grâce. Léon took his ice-axe out of his bag and drove it with all his strength into the fat bird's head. Surprised, the crow let go of its prey and turned its fury on Léon, slashing at him with its beak. He avoided the blows, taking care not to lose his balance. But the bird, already seeing him as another possible prey, flapped its wings, rose up a couple of inches and grasped him in its talons, forgetting to finish off the tit.

Léon was lifted high up into the air. He felt dizzy. It was no use him repeating: I love my family, love gives you wings, so I'm not afraid, he didn't believe a word of it. One should beware of metaphors. This time it was the end. The crow would split his skull with its beak or drop him from a hundred feet up until his body was shattered and it could gobble him up. But, hampered by the rain that was weighing its wings down, the bird didn't have time to get very high. Léon demonstrated the boldness of cowards who act without thinking. Still holding his ice-axe, he set about the crow's claws with it and hit them so hard, it let go of him. There was a kind of gaseous aureola blocking the horizon. He fell, prepared himself to die, broken on a metal ridge or a concrete wall. He landed on the net as if it were a trampoline, bouncing back up. Shivering with cold and fear, he crawled back to the kitchen window just in time to see that the tit had managed to extricate itself from the net and escape, despite its broken wing. With one last heave he pulled himself up to the half-open window, dropped onto the kitchen floor and fell asleep instantly, in a pool of water, bruised and with his palms and knees bleeding. He didn't even feel Furbelow licking him to warm him up.

17

Lazarus Rises from the Dead

He slept for fifteen hours solid. Then something remarkable happened: Léon rebelled. In a single night he banished all the humiliations and the torments he had suffered. A cat had saved him; he had saved a tit. It was time for him to save himself. How was it that for so long he had accepted being hounded without reacting?

Yesterday he had surpassed himself, why couldn't he surpass himself every day? A brush with death often gives people a new taste for life. Was he going to wait for his tormentors to come back from their holidays and let himself be rubbed out like a dirty mark on the wall just because they were his family? He climbed up onto Solange's dressing-table and examined himself in her swivel mirror. He was horrified at the way he looked; he felt dirty with his long beard, his tousled hair, his tattered clothes worthy of a vagabond. His scalp and arms were covered in scabs. He was disgusted at himself: he hadn't shrunk, he'd let himself go.

It was a revolution, a storm in the heart of the homunculus. He was seized with indignation. He was angry with himself for having been so weak, such a coward. He mocked himself, called himself names, slapped himself.

By midday his resolution was made. He gathered his things together, put them in a rucksack and waited for the arrival of the concierge, who would come to feed the cat in the early evening. Hardly had the man turned the key and opened the door than he had slipped out onto the landing.

Flight is the best vengeance.

Free! At last he was free!

What did the trials and tribulations he was going to encounter matter, he was his own master once more. He set off down the stairs cautiously. Each one was higher than he was, so he had to jump from one to the next, land on the carpet, stumble back against the riser and start again on the next one. They were sheer cliffs of the same height, terribly sheer. He might tumble down at any moment, bouncing from step to step, and break his bones. After the fourth floor it became easier. He found himself bounding down the stairs effortlessly, as in the days of his prime.

When he reached the third floor, he noticed a change: the window of the lift shaft, stained glass in the fin-de-siècle symbolist style, had come down to his level, the ceiling had lowered and the lift didn't seem so sizeable any more. And now he was skipping from one step to the next on one foot.

What was happening?

Quite simply: a miracle.

A miracle is the obverse of a catastrophe. It rewards those afflicted by it when a catastrophe strikes both innocent and guilty without distinction.

And this was the miracle: as he went away from the family home LÉON STARTED TO GROW AGAIN. And his clothes grew with him! For him going down meant regaining height and, above all, regaining his self-esteem. Léon had already lived through so many calamities and wonders that he wasn't particularly surprised at this phenomenon.

On the first floor, moving more and more easily with every step, he realised he was recovering his former body. He felt his head, raised his arms and looked at his feet that had gone off to the antipodes, far away from him. It almost made him feel dizzy. And it all held together, it didn't collapse like an over-ambitious building defying gravity. He had become the man he was eight years ago, five foot six inches tall.

All he had had to do was to move away from his family.

He refrained from excessive expressions of excitement or joy, concerned that he might be deceiving himself. He was probably dreaming, it was too much, it couldn't last. In a moment he was going to shrink again, contract, all wrinkled like the bellows of an accordion.

As he reached the ground floor, the street door opened and a joyful band charged into the hall. He recognised them at once: his children coming back from holiday, jostling each other, Solange holding the door open for them, while Dubbelviz was parking the car. He'd forgotten they were returning that day. If he'd stayed up there, visible to all, they would have dispatched him immediately with a flick of the hand, like some contemptible, shameful object. He shuddered at the thought. He couldn't believe that. Little children laughing so gaily don't become assassins, even out of thoughtlessness. To hear their charming tones, Solange's inflections, was heart-rending. They were his family, flesh of his flesh. It had all been a misunderstanding, they had to be given a second chance.

They were already in the lift taking them up to the fifth floor, chattering at the tops of their voices, excited because, from the scraps he heard, they were going off again a few days later to Italy, to stay in a house Dubbelviz had rented in Tuscany. In Tuscany! God, he really was pampering them, no expense spared. He heard Dubbelviz, weighed down with huge suitcases, get into the lift. He waited for a moment, then went back up the stairs, still stumbling on his enormous legs, amazed at covering so many miles so quickly. When he reached the top floor, he rang the bell.

The door hadn't been locked, he pushed it open and saw them through the glass door of the drawing room, to the left of the hall. The merry crew were sitting round the table having afternoon tea with lots of chattering and shouting, devouring Danish pastries, chocolate milk and biscuits. They were tanned, rested, looking radiant all of them, with a wealth of flowing locks bleached by the sun. Professor Dubbelviz, sunburnt as an old seadog, had let his pepper-and-salt beard grow and was dandling Bérénice on his knee. Léon cleared his throat and was almost astonished that he managed to utter these words: 'Solange, children, it's me, it's Daddy, I've come back.'

He took three hesitant steps towards them, all too aware of his dirty, ugly state. The shriek of horror they gave when they saw him! They wouldn't have screamed any the less if they'd seen the devil in person. Their mouths hung open, their spoons sank back onto the table, they stared at him, a circle of abject terror. The twins hid under the table, the older two fled into Solange's arms and Dubbelviz, trembling and disbelieving, rose to his imposing height to bar his way.

Something strange had happened. Those who had seemed fearsome now seemed harmless. They, at least the adults, were still taller than him but inoffensive. Léon had an ace up his sleeve: he was the man who could grow and shrink in a flash, like a sorcerer. That just made him all the more frightening in the eyes of his family. He repeated: 'Children, it's me, Léon, your father, I've got my old height back. I'll tell you all about it.'

Dubbelviz, deathly pale, muttered, 'Who are you, monsieur, what are you doing in my apartment?'

'And you, monsieur, how dare you live in *my* apartment?'

Solange felt faint and collapsed on the floor while the kids ran off in terror. The horrible Josiane, who had come running from the kitchen, crossed herself three times when she saw Léon and disappeared down the stairs. The two men bent down to help Solange, their heads clashing as they did so. Dubbelviz thought he was being attacked and stepped back, putting up his hands in front of his face to protect himself. Léon took Solange under the armpits to pull her onto the settee, found her rather heavy and saw from the bulge swelling her linen tunic that she was with child again.

He was thunderstruck. He had believed he was the only one with the right to make her pregnant, the only one entitled to make that silky stomach swell up whenever he liked. She opened her eyes, in which hatred had overcome fear, and struggled to stop him helping her. The prodigal's return was not welcome. Unable to bear her look, Léon staggered back, and started to babble incoherently. In a few words he told them about his life during the last few months, his hideout in the treasures of world literature, how he had saved the tit, his final metamorphosis on the staircase. As he spoke, went into detail, he seemed even more insane. Dubbelviz tried a rational question: 'But... I... thought that... you were dead.'

'You tried, I know... I don't hold it against you.'

Meanwhile the kids had come back and were standing in the doorway staring at him, round-eyed. He held out his arms to them, telling himself he would have more chance with his offspring and went to kiss them. These former giants, whose brutality or passing crazes he had still been afraid of the previous day, begged him, blubbering, not to kill them and scattered like sparrows frightened by a firecracker. He tried to put himself in their place, remembering his own reactions when he'd been tiny. He should have shaved before coming to see them, put on a clean suit. He must look like a ghost. He heard Baptiste tell his mother – from a distance – to call the police; the boy, covered in freckles, had a snub nose that gave him a mischievous air. Josiane, the virago, who had returned brandishing a crucifix, suggested the services of an exorcist she knew.

'Monsieur,' Solange said in a toneless voice, 'the man you claim to be died a long time ago. Please leave or I'll call the police.'

'But Solange, it's me, Léon, your Léon, who gave you four children, Baptiste, Betty, Boris and Bérénice. And there's a fact that I can't have invented: I've one shoulder lower than the other, you remember? Give me a holiday photo where I'm stripped to the waist.'

But his face had disappeared from all the picture frames on the mantelpiece, rubbed out or cut out with a razor blade. Since he had rarely gone on the tables or higher shelves in his midget days he hadn't noticed that all trace of him had been removed while Dubbelviz was everywhere: in a city suit, in his pyjamas, in shorts with his hairy thighs. It was another blow: he'd been expunged, he'd never existed.

Solange quickly recovered her composure. She sent the children out, closed the glass door of the dining room and took an envelope full of orange and green notes out of a desk.

'Take that and go. I don't want to know how you managed to survive. I don't care. Just clear off.'

She spat out the words. Underneath the holiday tan her skin was mottled with pale patches, her chin was quivering. A few stands of grey tarnished her auburn hair. The amazon who used to mesmerise him had broadened out. He put it down to her pregnancy. Had he confused size with beauty?

'Fuck off, d'you hear. Tell him Daniel, come on, tell him,

throw him out. You're the man round here, aren't you?'

Dubbelviz, paralysed with fear, was keeping well clear, wringing his hands in embarrassment and letting her get on with it. The six-foot mastodon was shaking in his shoes.

'How dare you come back after everything you've done to us?' Solange said.

Her anger made her ugly, she flushed to the roots of her hair and her eyelid was twitching like a loose shutter in the wind.

'You ruined my reputation, made me look ridiculous in the eyes of my family. My friends were revolted at the idea of a beautiful woman like me sharing my bed with a runt, letting him have his dirty little way with me. They urged me to leave you, to find a man who was my equal. I held on, love helped me to overcome all these trials: I refused to see you the way you were, a tumour at my breast, a festering sore. I ignored the mockery, the warnings. As time passed I wanted to expunge you, what I felt for you was a mixture of pity and affection in which pity was by far the stronger. But I made it my duty not to abandon you, despite your disability you had given me four splendid children. I was sure things would turn out all right, that you'd grow again one day, like a vigorous plant.'

Out of breath, she stopped and asked Dubbelviz to fetch her a glass of water. He dashed off, all too happy to oblige. She collapsed into an armchair, exhausted, and went on in a low voice:

'I wasn't wrong, I was just mistaken about the timing. The smaller you became the more you spread discord in the family, taking advantage of your size to stand up to me, turn the little ones against me. It was too easy for you to wriggle out of things while I had everything on my shoulders. There are limits to what a loving woman can put up with. For a long time men were afraid of me, afraid they might dissolve, evaporate at my side. There were not very flattering rumours about me going round but I managed to dispel them. You've brought nothing but suffering and hardship to this family. Your children were ashamed of you. I hate to think what would have become of us if Daniel hadn't decided to share our life, that is, to save us. My parents are old and ill.'

All of a sudden, her face contorted with anger, she leapt up out of the chair and stood face to face with him.

'And now you dare to come back, all simpering, expecting everything to be the same again? I don't want to know what happened to you, Léon. You don't exist any more, you're just a mistake creation made, everyone's forgotten you. I love Dubbelviz, see, I'm pregnant by him, he's the man in my life and the children are already calling him Daddy.'

She was exaggerating her anger, her cutting words lost their edge, like a little child's fists pummelling an adult's belly. He felt sorry for her. She paused, breathless, almost suffocated by her harangue. In a whisper, she said, 'Please. Take the money and go away, I beg you. I won't report you for forcible entry.'

She slumped on the chair, sobbing. Dubbelviz, a glass of water in his hand, ran over to comfort her. She wasn't malicious, she was an unhappy woman feeling sorry for herself, for the ruin of her ambitions. She wanted to save her own skin. She made Léon feel sad.

The children, who had recovered from their fright and were clustered round the glass door to the drawing room, the twins with their noses flattened against the panes by the pressure of the bigger ones behind them, watched the scene open-mouthed. Their flabbergasted looks expressed astonishment more than hostility. They watched Léon, perhaps hoping for a fight between him and Dubbelviz and that the Big Barrel of Beef would get a drubbing. They were wrong about the target.

For Léon, seeing the gang of snotty-nosed brats who had driven him up the wall for so many years, couldn't resist: rolling up his sleeves, he took their trousers down and gave each one a good hiding there and then. It was a nasty trick, perhaps, but it did him good. And since Baptiste was still his favourite, he gave him a double portion. They all howled, except Baptiste, who didn't bat an eyelid and stared at him between smacks with a cheeky, almost admiring look. Dubbelviz lowered his gaze discreetly and Solange fainted again. It was the most violent thrashing Léon had ever handed out in his whole life; he smacked the plump bottoms of those well-fed kids so hard that the palms of his hands stung. Feeling better, he took the wad of banknotes and slammed the door behind him without looking back.

Epilogue

A few minutes later he came out onto the square facing their apartment; it was over six months since he'd been out in the open air. He swayed under the onslaught of the light, almost choked. He had to get used to his new body and stumbled along, gauging distances poorly, thinking everything was closer or farther away than it really was.

He flopped down on a bench, put his head in his hands and cried like a little child, unconcerned about the stares of the passers-by, kids, who were being taken for a walk by their nannies, pointing at him. Too many things had strained his nerves to breaking point. They were tears of joy and grief at the same time, as he said farewell to one period and looked forward to a new existence. As he was wiping his eyes, a little bird came hopping along in front of him. Its left wing was broken in two and hung down, hampering it. Despite that, it was chirping, singing its two notes, always the same ones, a harmonious refrain. By its black head Léon recognised it as the little tit he'd saved from the crow's talons. It still had need of him. He held out his forefinger and, flexing it carefully, moved it into the hollow of his hand. The bird cheeped, trusting him. What a pair they made, the two of them: the outcast and the cripple. He felt the envelope in his pocket. He had enough money to have the tit seen to by a vet, buy himself a new suit and clean underwear, and take a room in a hotel. He had to clean himself up if he didn't want the police to arrest him for vagrancy. He still had his degrees, his knowledge, he would take up his profession again, invent some story to explain his absence. For example, he'd tell people he'd shrunk. No one would believe him. Now and then he'd see how his children were doing.

He'd go back in a few days for the cat.

The curse wouldn't affect him again.

He set off through the streets of Paris, his twittering companion on his shoulder, pecking at the threadbare cloth of his jacket, warbling its head off.

He felt quite perky at the thought of the bad things he'd avoided, the good things to come. There were any number of stunning women between five foot and five foot five.

He would remain a man of average height.

He would never be a little husband again.

Afterword

My Little Husband belongs to a literary and pictorial tradition that has always fascinated me, that of transformations of the body – distension, increase or reduction in size – that goes from Rabelais to Marcel Aymé and includes Swift, Voltaire, Balzac, Lewis Carroll, F. S. Fitzgerald, Richard Matheson and many others. It is equally represented in the twentieth-century strip cartoon, from Winsor McCay's *Little Nemo* to Hergé's *The Crab with the Golden Claws*, not forgetting the many post-war cartoons with giant insects resulting from atomic explosions, huge babies feeding their mothers, miniaturised adults cradled in the arms of ravishingly full-bosomed creatures.

At a time when mankind, so scientists assure us, is constantly increasing in size, *My Little Husband* takes up, from a different perspective, the theme of regression I have already treated in *The Divine Child* (Little, Brown, 1994): a foetus, informed about the problems of the world while still in the womb, refuses to be born and stays permanently with mummy. *The Divine Child* itself came from one page of my first novel, *Monsieur Tac* (Sagittaire, 1976), the story of a man who suffers constant changes of weight, mood and height as he goes through the alphabet: at the letter B for birth his mother, realising her baby is refusing to come out, sends a gynaecologist inside her to find the refusenik. But he hides behind an ovary, ambushes the scientist and pushes him into his mother's bladder, where he drowns.